THE THING ABOUT SPACE

A Novella

the thing about space

shaun powell

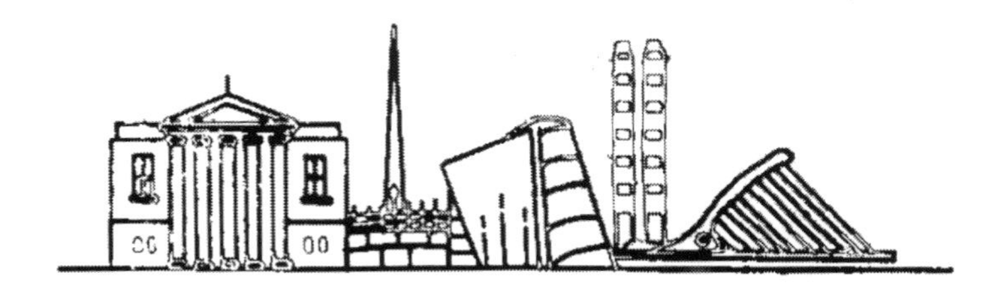

the thing about space

ISBN: 9798695865936
Imprint: Independently published

The characters and events portrayed in this book are fictitious. Any similarity to real persons, living or dead, is coincidental and not intended by the author.

*Front cover design by: Ellen Jones per @_ellustrate_*
*Interior illustration by: Laura Sheridan per @lauraelizabethdesign_*

the thing about space

To Norma

And

The Aliens

the thing about space

The Familiar Stranger

She stands a silhouette
To the falling light,
Soft silk, swollen eyes
From the endless night

A burning mind
Sits cold inside,
Restless

Thorn and thistle,
Alluringly bright,
Mysterious light
I dream the night,
I see her light

Karl McMurry

the thing about space

one

I had been staring at the sun for too long. Or, at least, that's how it felt sometimes. She was the first thing I saw every morning, scorched into the back of my eyelids like a blister. On better days she was barely there, a remnant of a dream that seemed to dissolve with consciousness. On other days, though, she was as dazzling and defined as the star itself. A beacon to guide me. A supernova to destroy me.

Before I could spare her a thought this morning however, I was greeted with a pounding headache and a dry throat. The combination roused me like a delirious lover but was about as graceful as a bunch of children jumping on my bed. *Wake up! Wake up!* It said as I coiled and groaned in a groggy limbo.

The retaliation was from a cheap bottle of merlot. I'd drained it some hours ago, relishing that fleeting moment in the middle of the night wherein which the usually busy street below my apartment became desolate. It's corpse on my bedside locker taunted me, the bottle glowing opaquely in a bright morning light that barraged through a gap in the curtains.

I forced myself up, back cracking like the spine of an old book, and repositioned a pillow against the wooden headboard. My laptop was still ajar on my bed but had snuck away from me during the night, was about an inch from slipping to the floor. I lifted it in front of me – not so fast, sucker – and gingerly caressed it back to life, not wanting to upset it before we even began. The screen illuminated, shocking my tired eyes.

Someone once said that the best time to write was as soon as you woke up. Something to do with that part of your brain – the part where other worlds lived, waiting to be discovered and exposed – being its most active during the hours when most normal people would be downing bitter coffee and combatting sleep's hangover with a shower. I actually think I was the fool who said it, funnily enough. A quote from an interview with some b-list women's magazine – the kind that came free with The Irish Times – back when people didn't just care about what I wrote but what I *said* too. Imagine that.

I exited out of the browser pages I had open from last night – an email from Fiona reminding me of our meeting later today – and pulled up the dreaded manuscript. It was exactly the way I'd left it. In fact, it hadn't changed in months. Not since the day all normality packed up and forsake me like a fed up husband, sneaking with it my ability to write. And maybe a little of my self-restraint, too.

I sighed. Long and heavy, rattled with agitation.

The text cursor blinked at me but I remained still, continuing my winning streak in this twisted staring contest we'd been having since late January. I waited long enough to know that this was definitely not happening today, fingers hovering over the keyboard as though the slightest touch would zap me.

I looked around the room for inspiration, like words were just there to grab, floating in the ether, circulating like those tiny plates in a sushi restaurant. I found none of course and gladly became distracted by the sudden hushed sound of movement in the hallway.

After five days in the guest bedroom – a modest room I'd surrendered in February to Bunker, an online marketplace for lodging and homestays – the Canadians were leaving. They hauled their outrageously large suitcases along the floor, their shadows soon appearing in the crack beneath my door. They stalled there, and I felt their hesitation. Knock to bid me farewell or leave without a word and be deemed impolite? Thankfully, they chose the latter, and I didn't think any less of them for it. In fact, I was relieved and in no hurry to subject them – or myself – to the awkward small talk that arose during checkout.

"Keep in touch, won't you?"

"Of course, yeah! Have a safe journey!"

I watched the long strokes of their shadows disappear, my shoulders unhooking from my ears after the front door shut behind them. Five minutes later, my phone vibrated. A notification from Bunker confirming their checkout. It was accompanied with a five-star rating and a small paragraph that read:

Clare's place along the quays was perfect for our Dublin getaway! Although we didn't get to see much of our host, she was very welcoming and always quick to respond. Thank you, Clare! PS – we left you a little something!

Either it was a safe bet or they'd noticed the graveyard in my room. Out of bed now and in the kitchen, I discovered that the Canadians had left a bottle of wine next to the spare keys and, although my stomach clenched like a baby's tiny fist at the thought of alcohol, I'd be glad of it later.

They were sweet people, I guess. Quiet. I kind of wish I'd gotten to know them, gotten to know any of the people that came across my apartment on Bunker. However, I always learned more about the guests from the state they left the room in. Take Les and Lilly, for example; the Canadians were tidy people, probably had an immaculate home back in Vancouver, the kind of place all their interesting, handsome friends preferred to come to for game nights and barbeques. They were thoughtful too, had even gone to the trouble of stripping the bed and folding the towels, their efforts almost loathsome.

While spreading clean sheets onto the mattress later that morning, I decided I'd give Les and Lilly five stars too, if not for their manners and lack of lingering, then for the gift they'd left me. Maybe I'd even adorn my review with a smiley face, apologize for my absence. I'd blame it on work and of course they'd understand, as would any potential guests lurking in the comments. Big time writer in the city working hard on the follow up to her debut, so successful and loaded she's had to the pimp out the spare room online to make the mortgage repayments each month. Completely acceptable.

By noon, the room was back to normal, immaculate and cosy, though it couldn't shake that eerie, show house vibe it had about it now.

I smoothed the creases from the duvet, sprayed some air freshener and fanned out the tourist guides and the sheet of house-rules. No smoking, no parties, no unprovoked conversations with the host that may cause her to scream internally. The last one might not have been typed up and laminated, but I made it clear by my evasiveness in every interaction I've had with a visitor thus far.

Before retreating, I noticed that the painting above the bed had deviated. Actually, it was exactly the way it should be: completely straight and law-abiding. But that wasn't the way the artist wanted it. Roisin had originally hung her painting crooked, explaining to me how it made more sense to be viewed askew. Though, I always thought this was a comical attempt to camouflage her lack of DIY skills.

"Well, how does it look?" she had asked me in front of the painting, not a year ago. Paling streaks of paint stained her *Repeal* sweater, the badge of honour she'd worn every other day during that momentous time in Ireland.

"I think it would look great if I had a broken neck," I replied, earning a playful slap on the arm. "No, I'm only messing. It's beautiful, Roisin."

"But?" She had sensed my scepticism.

"*But*… what is it exactly?" I couldn't for the life of me make out what I was looking at. The painting was bold and colourful, something you'd see in one of those discreet art galleries in town, a neutral, echoey room Roisin would often drag me to.

Paintings and sculptures were always hard for me to *get*. Words were easier. They literally told you, almost absolutely, what they were, what they wanted you to feel.

"It's us, Clare," she revealed, crossing her arms and admiring her work. "It's us and all the space in-between."

The memory was like a bruise in my mind. I couldn't apply too much pressure to it or risk further damage.

I stood on the bed and tilted the painting again.

Peace restored.

two

After a paltry brunch, little wet footprints trailed me from the shower back to my bedroom. I confronted the mirror inside, began the silent conversation between my appearance and I.

Something had shifted recently. It was unavoidable. The deterioration was nagging at me like a loose tooth, one that threatened to come free and expose parts I thought had been jettisoned in my adolescence.

The weight had fallen from me first. Little bits here and there, like Hansel and Gretel dropping breadcrumbs along a perilous road. My hair had gone limp too, eyes hollow and anchored with such heavy, purple bags that I could almost hear mam say, *You'd be fit to take the shopping home with those things, Clare!*

The girl staring back at me looked defeated, a houseplant that might be beautiful if only you'd remember to water the damn thing, and much like Roisin's painting, I believed I appeared much better when viewed a certain way now. Perhaps with your eyes scrunched and unfocused.

I was rustling a towel around my head when the buzzer rang. The abrupt sound flooded my quiet apartment with the particular dread of an unexpected visitor. Dashing to the window, I peeled back the curtain to spy the caller, felt the intensity of peeking at a textbook during a class test.

Christ, I was becoming more and more like a character from a Hitchcock movie.

Let's go down there and find out what's buried in that garden!

I didn't recognize the woman, found her sudden arrival into my life just as peculiar as the pink dye that bled from the end of her relaxed ponytail. She must have pressed the wrong apartment number, I thought. She could even live in this building and simply forgot her fob-key. Yes, that'd be it. Happens all the time. Someone would let her in any second now.

The curtain fell back into place and I returned to the edge of the bed, started on tackling the knots in my hair. Thoughts turned to my imminent appointment with Fiona and…

The buzzer again. Longer this time, fuelled with impatience. I stomped out of the room, retracing my footsteps past the bathroom, steam still spilling from it, and to the hall door.

"Hello?" I said into the speaker system on the wall, the word climbing from my mouth as though I was announcing myself in a house believed to be haunted.

"Hey, it's Zoe," came the woman from the other end. "Your message on Bunker said to ring this number?" Her voice was soft and sweet, dancing with a northern Irish accent that could turn the most dull statements into cheery melodies. It didn't belong to the girl I saw from the window but to my favourite primary school teacher or to a cold call agent I actually *did* have a spare five minutes for, if just to hear her speak.

I squeezed my eyes shut, racked my brain. There was something from last night, clouded now but still discernible, like driving in the rain.

A last minute booking request. Yes, I remember now. A bit glazed and brimming with deceitful confidence, I had approved Zoe's request with little thought.

"Shite," she said then. "I haven't got the wrong place, have I?"

"No, you're fine," I replied, buzzing her in. "Come on up. Fifth floor."

I raced back to my room in search of clothes, found little mountains of them littering my room as if a handful of people had been raptured. By now, Zoe would be at the elevator, potentially ascending, and there I was wrapped in a towel, skin still slick.

I resorted to yesterday's outfit, dragging cold denim along my wet legs, wrestling into a loose, mauve sweater. I barely had time to pull on socks before she announced herself with three eager knocks.

At the door again, I braced myself, opened it quickly as though pulling a band-aid.

"Hi!" she exclaimed immediately, her enthusiasm matching that of an old friend I hadn't seen in years; I worried she was going to launch into a hug right away, nearly stumbled into one myself out of anxiety.

Up close, Zoe was unearthly beautiful, a bright smile capped with pinchable, who's a good girl dimples, her skin so porcelain I couldn't tell whether she was wearing make-up or if she'd just never had a restless night in her life.

"Hey, Zoe. Nice to meet you," I replied, then noticed how she was lingering on the threshold, a vampire awaiting an invitation. "Come in, come in! Don't mind the state of the place." Or the state of me, I should've added. Next to her, I looked like the before picture from some miraculous makeover show – tonight, Matthew, I'm going to be... *presentable!*

"Thanks," she said, bumbling by me into the hallway, officially joining my world. The smell of summer, of fresh, green air and slight perspiration masked with a delicate deodorant chased her and filled the small space. It was a pleasant scent, a familiar scent; I had a small treasure buried in my bottom drawer that carried that very smell, an old shirt belonging to Roisin.

"Oh, what a day," Zoe sighed as I shut the door, allowing her weekend bag, pregnant with clothes and shoes and what appeared to be a hairdryer, to fall by her feet. "What is it with men not understanding the leg space rule on public transport?"

I laughed and agreed – *I know right!* – but then it became quiet for a moment, the walls of the hallway closing in with each passing second of silence. You'd assume I'd be used to this kind of thing but, even after months of alternating housemates, I'd only greeted a handful of them upon arrival. This was unfamiliar territory to me.

"You're down from Belfast, right?" I finally said, wringing my brain like a damp sponge, earning little droplets of information from our brief conversation on Bunker last night. Quiet girl. From Belfast. One-night stay. "How was the journey?"

I walked into the living area, twitched my head for Zoe to follow.

"Aye," she said, joining me in the kitchen, the word folding in on itself at the back of her mouth like a wave, "it took a lifetime, but it wasn't too bad now."

"That bus ride is pretty grim though, isn't it?"

I wanted to hear her say that word again, to pull a string on the back of her body over and over until it lost its charm.

Aye. Aye. Aye.

"I took the Belfast Express down, actually."

My chest tightened, breath freezing in my mouth and lingering on my lips like a kiss. "Right. Of course," I managed to exhale, a shaky whisper. "The train." I felt as though I was on one myself – one that had, without warning, shot backwards into a dark tunnel.

Sensing a mysterious change in the room, Zoe shifted uncomfortably and then acknowledged her surroundings, saying, “Beautiful place you’ve got here.” Her eyes fell onto the dining area sandwiched between the kitchen and the living room, then to the large floor-to-ceiling windows beyond that offered an unrivalled view of the River Liffey. “I’ve heard the horror stories of renting in Dublin, but this isn’t too bad at all.”

I had to tease myself back, coaxing my senses to me like a wary kitten.

“It’s actually mine,” I quickly said, grateful for a change in conversation, though not as self-effacing as I wanted to come across to a stranger. “Which really just means I’m under the bank’s thumb and not a landlord’s.”

“Aye, I understand. Different thumbs, same hands, is it?”

“Something like that,” I said with a grin.

We caught eyes for a moment. I looked back to the kitchen.

“Would you like a cup of tea or anything?” I said, twisting towards the kettle in a hurry. She refused politely, but I flicked it to life anyway, if not for an excuse to look busy and courteous, then for a sound to salve the room.

Pouring boiling water over the tea bag for myself, I asked, “So what is it that brings you down, anyway?” She didn’t respond, and I turned back to find Zoe wandering towards the window, her movements about my apartment assured and effortless. Balletic almost.

Who was this girl? I wondered as I stood behind her then, clasping the mug.

The familiar ache to know her inside out was immediate. Like a fancy book cover catching my attention from a shelf, I wanted to devour her story, to live it all – her friends, her family, the movies she liked, the men or women she loved – and then regurgitate it into my own work someday.

Zoe pressed herself against the glass like a child in an aquarium and said, “You can see Conolly’s Bridge from here.” She was so amazed, so confident, but also so, so mistaken; I hated to burst her bubble, but no self-respecting Irish person could let that slide.

“*O’Connell* Bridge,” I corrected, timidly moving closer to her, wondering why I feel so out of place in my own home.

"And that's actually the Samuel Beckett Bridge you're looking at."

"Ah, don't shoot!" she pleaded, holding up her arms.

I allowed a tittered laugh, took a sip of tea. The sun was shining right onto us, warming my skin and most likely washing me out. But it illuminated Zoe, made little galaxies of her kaleidoscopic eyes.

Dublin looked beautiful today, the kind of rare summer afternoon that forced you to reconsider any thoughts you ever had about leaving.

The sky above was periwinkle blue, a vast expanse that would surely inspire some beautiful poetry and encourage days spent under it in Stephen's Green, watching as it wanes to pink. Sparse, frothy clouds decorated the blue, seemed to meander about the place without a care in the world, whilst, down below, the city centre streets were growing busy again.

Cars, vans and congested, double-decker buses jammed the North Wall Quay roads. They filed into the lanes, stalling for a moment as the traffic lights switched, and then surged on again, engines purring.

On the cobble pavements adjacent, eager visitors on city bikes and scantly dressed teenagers loitered along the river where, on the shimmering water, one of those Viking themed, touristy boats proudly soared by.

"Look at them," said Zoe as a crew of middle-aged men roared from the boat. They were hardly pedalling fast enough to keep up with a lone rower who eventually overtook them. "That looks like a geg, doesn't it?"

She was smiling, so I assumed a *geg* was Northern Irish for a good time.

I cleared my throat, took another sip of tea. "It is good craic, to be honest," I admitted, swallowing hard. "I actually did it once with my roommate, years ago."

I was walking on broken glass here; I had to be cautious. Despite having swept most of the night away now, a prickly splinter still remained from the wreckage.

It was Roisin's twenty-first birthday and a handful of mates from college, and I had rented one of those boats as part of an unconventional celebration plan. We'd start there, on the water, using the boat as our pre-drinking location, and then move on to a karaoke bar on South William street before a night in some smoggy club in town.

Though nearly a decade ago now, I can still summon the sound of laughter from that boat, can still see the look on Roisin's broiling face as she struggled to cycle anymore, cursing at the lot of us through theatrical gasps for breath.

"Guys, I can't," Roisin had panted, the dark water chopping around us. "I'm gonna have a heart attack."

"Come on, Ro!" came Jack Murray, one of our classmates from Trinity. In hindsight, he was probably doing the most to keep the boat moving that night, his legs and arms like a titan's. "Pretend you're pedalling towards Tubridy – that'll keep you going."

"*Eff* off, Murray," Roisin snapped back, her cheeks burning as we laughed.

Although she made no secret of her admiration for Ireland's late-night talk show host, it was always a source of amusement in our group and had become a regular and reliable quip. She literally made me pinkie-promise I wouldn't breathe a word of the Ryan Tubridy mosaic she kept in her room, even though it reminded me of granny and her ghoulish portrait of Jesus Christ.

It would be a promise I'd come to break, only after she broke her own.

"I didn't know you had a roommate," said Zoe, and the memory of that night burned away like the end of a film roll. "Is she here?"

The mug slipped from my hands, exploded around my feet.

Zoe jolted backwards, eyes wild, brows connecting with her fringe.

"Crap!" I exclaimed, apologising as I dropped to my knees to collect the fragments. My skin flushed under my clothes from embarrassment, hands quivering with a thousand thoughts – not one of them linear. I didn't dare look up but could feel Zoe's eyes on me, burrowing into my back.

What must she think of me? I thought. I could see the Bunker guest review already: *pleasant views, demented host,* it would probably say.

Zoe was down in an instant, however, and she began gathering the sharp pieces into her own little stockpile. “Don’t worry about it,” she said, and with that voice as soft as cotton, her words almost succeeded in their attempt to dispel any humiliation.

Almost.

“Excuse me. I’m just… it’s just…” but I couldn’t ferret out the words. I’d spent so long turning them over in my head that they didn’t even *feel* like native words anymore. Trying to say them aloud was like trying to speak with a mouth full of marbles.

I pinched up the remnants of the mug I’d stacked and then took Zoe’s, pressing a little too hard on an edge; it pierced my palm.

“Ouch,” I said, wincing. A worm of scarlet blood came wriggling from the wound, tunnelled down my palm like the tiny lines on a map.

I brought my hand up and held it between us, reminiscent of a Shakespearian actor seeking answers. To bleed or not to bleed?

"You go look after that," Zoe said then. "I'll sort this out."

Nodding, I returned to my feet, pausing for a moment next to her.

There's a certain safety in being alone, I thought, a comforting freedom completely bereft of expectations and responsibilities. I'd grown accustomed to that liberty, even quite fond of it, framing myself within it like a ship in one of those impossible, glass bottles. Which made me wonder; was my new guest – as beguiling as she was – an unassuming threat to that freedom, a Trojan horse I irresponsibly hauled into my new, vigilant world?

I retreated to the bathroom, pressing the door shut behind me. The emptiness of the room and its promise of peace and privacy enveloped me immediately, welcoming me home as if it were a loved one at an airport.

Away from Zoe and shielded from her curiosity, relief trickled over me like a sweet, hot syrup. The force in my sails slackened, and I allowed them to come down once again. Here – alone – I could just drift for a little while.

I turned to the sink. A twist of the spokes and cold water gushed from the faucet. Unfurling my hand against the stream, the gash twinged from the sudden disturbance, rich red blood diluting in my palm like a tiny pool of summer fruits squash.

Tilting my hand over, the build-up of rusted water whirled down the drain and eventually the flow ran clear. I slung a nervous look into the mirror above the sink and then away, eyes stinging. Something was blossoming in me, a familiar but loathsome sensation that I could sense coming on. An inconvenient, emotional sneeze.

I tried to suppress it, tried to punch the feeling back down to my gut where it had been nesting all day, all week, all month, but it was pointless. My vision divided from my thoughts – a deep pensiveness that was about as decipherable as Russian cursive – and my stomach clenched, bracing itself.

Without deciding to, I began to sob.

My hands quickly rose to my mouth as if to catch the abrupt whimpers and stuff them back in. But there were too many. Emotions seemed to be scattering from every orifice in my body, weeping from every pore on my skin, seizing their one chance of escaping the deep well I'd been drowning them in.

I froze and started to panic; what if one of my freed cries had crept through the crack under the door, permeating the walls, and travelled to Zoe in the living room?

I waited with bated breath for a sign – a footstep, the creak of a floorboard – chest tightening like a vacuum pack. My hands were a muzzle around my mouth, my jaw beneath it trembling as I continued to cry in silence, in secrecy.

I could only hope that the falling water, the grunting pipes it came from, somehow managed to muffle the sounds of my shame.

Despite my concern, however, Zoe never came to the door. Either I'd gotten better at the whole covert misery thing or she actually *did* hear and decided it wasn't worth the bother.

Don't ask me which one of those scenarios I preferred.

When I finally gathered myself and left the bathroom – flushing the toilet behind me for appearances – I found Zoe in the kitchen. She looked none the wiser, emptying the remains of the broken mug into the bin.

"All sorted?" she asked.

I smiled, ran my unspoiled hand along my jumper.

"Good as new."

three

An escape route presented itself whilst showing Zoe around her room.

"Christ, is that the time already?" I said, looking at my phone's screen with a little too much bewilderment. "I better get going here. I'm running late for a thing in town."

Technically not a lie. There *was* a meeting in town, I just wasn't running late for it at all. Some lies aren't only white or black, I think, but grey and beneficial for both parties. We tell them every day and if you say you don't, you're most likely lying to yourself.

Anyhow, I arrived at my agent's office on Harcourt Street – a symmetrical brown-stone Georgian building with a royal blue door – twenty minutes before expected. I even had time to cycle through Stephen's Green, assimilating with the rest of its carefree, sun-drenched colonists as I cruised along the paths like some happy, healthy woman from a multi-vitamin commercial.

Who's lying to themselves now, hey?

At the black, wrought-iron railings, I clamped my bike and ascended the four steps to the blue door, pressed the buzzer there. Behind me, the warning bell of the green-line Luas, Dublin's tram system, chimed as it slithered by. The southbound commuters inside swayed, faces buried into phones and iPads and newspapers. Though in its adolescence now, the Luas still felt new to me and yet, like the Spire impaling the sky from O'Connell Street, I couldn't imagine Dublin City without it.

"Please tell me you're here to bludgeon me with that, Clare," said Fiona Kelly as I crept into her office on the second floor, heavy helmet hanging from my wrist.

My literary agent was tucked into her enormous pine desk, arched over a manuscript like an archaeologist unsure

if their latest discovery was treasure or jus
dirt.

Judging from the strain on her face, I could assume which way she was leaning.

“Bad day?” I said with a grin, hanging up my things.

Even though I enjoyed Fiona’s company, had spent some of the best days of my writing career in that office, my stomach hovered with dread. As much as I’d like it to be, this was not a social call. However, I wasn’t sure if it was strictly business either.

Fiona sighed, the base of her swivel chair groaning as she leant back, and lifted her glasses from her face as if they were heavy. She forced the frame through her dense, blonde hair, which I noticed had recently started to flirt with grey.

“If I have to read one more submission about an American exchange student at Trinity,” she said, rubbing her eyes, “I’m retiring early.”

“Hey, at least it’s not vampires.”

“At least it’s not vampires!”

Fiona fluttered her hand towards the two chairs in front of her then and I took my usual seat, began nervously tugging at a loose piece of thread on it.

This was where I sat when I handed Fiona the draft of what would become my debut novel. This was where I sat when I first heard the words – at least in relation to me – *two-book deal* and *number one bestseller.* And now there I was, in the very chair I'd sat in a hundred times, the picture of a school child about to be yelled at by their principal.

We swapped formalities initially, a tennis match in courtesy that I had surprising stamina for.

She told me about her new assistant, a recent graduate named Ellen, who she feared was over-qualified to be fetching coffee and answering submission e-mails. I told her that's how it was in Dublin now and then asked how her kids were doing. Leanne was doing great as always, she said, had even taken up piano recently, but Conor…

"A condom!" she exclaimed. "Right there on his locker like a coaster, Clare."

"At least he's being safe," I said, and she nearly choked.

“Safe? Let’s see how safe he’ll be on the streets after I kick him out.”

Back and forth we went like that for a while. I’d have said anything, talked for hours about her teenage sons sex life, to keep the conversation from turning to the inevitable. Ultimately though, Fiona cut to the chase, finally satisfied in her efforts to prime me.

“Look, Clare,” she said, fussing with some papers on her desk, realigning a stapler. “You know I’ve always been a champion of your work.”

“Of course, yeah.”

“Lately, however, there’s been some…” she paused to find the right word, one that wouldn’t completely dismantle the rickety scaffolding opposite her. “Well, there’s been some concerns from people outside of this room.”

“Do you mean doubts, Fiona?”

She half shrugged. “Fine,” she admitted. “There have been doubts.”

I didn’t know what to say. How could I tell her that writing wasn’t coming easy to me anymore, that it was a chore on most days? What had once been as natural as breathing was now like wading through the thickest mud.

I was sinking. I knew it. She knew it. The publishers obviously knew it.

"You haven't been yourself lately," Fiona declared. "It's showing in your work, Clare. At least in the little work I *have* seen."

She let that sit between us, an ominous tarot card I didn't quite know the meaning of.

Looking her in the eye was dangerous then. They were too caring, too curious. Fiona had this look about her I'd seen only a handful of times before; the night when, at fourteen years old, my mother found me retching my dinner into the toilet bowl because nothing tasted as good as skinny felt; the morning when I'd turned to Jack Murray in bed and said, "This doesn't feel right anymore," and he didn't even put up a fight but just stared. What were their eyes searching for in me? Answers? Remorse?

"I know," I mumbled, head hanging.

Being aware of it yourself, the black dagger poking from your chest, is one thing, but hearing someone else acknowledge it is a sharp twist.

Not one to hold back though – a trait I usually admired – Fiona brought up the deadlines I've strayed from and the starved chapters I'd been sending her for feedback. But I was thinking about what she had said before, about how I haven't been myself.

I always wondered what that might be like, to undoubtedly know who you are despite all the distortions and distractions. Underneath the rubble and in-between the vines that thicken with age, with experience, to still see oneself. And what of the people who didn't, the ones who looked inward and saw multitudes? Or worse, the ones that delved into themselves and found nothing or no one at all?

She'd hit the nail on the head; whatever version of myself I'd assembled, the traits and talents I'd nurtured or abandoned respectively over the years, was long lost. What started as a detour had developed into an entirely new route, but turning back was impossible. Conversely, looking forward was daunting.

Maybe I just had to accept that this is where I was now.

"I finished a chapter this morning," I said, the lie gusting from my mouth in a desperate attempt to save face. "A good chapter. A meaty one. I think you'll be thrilled with it."

Fiona looked dubious but humoured me.

"And the first draft?" she said, an eyebrow raising. It was less of a question and more of a challenge. A command. There *will* be a first draft, it really said.

"Almost done. A week. Two, tops."

Those weren't grey lies I was telling. They were coal black and filthy, smearing my hands. I felt ashamed, worthy of having a crowd hurl rotten tomatoes at me until I was drenched red. But I'd do it, I vowed. I'd nail myself to my desk for the next two weeks if that's what it took.

four

"Did you hear that, Clare? They can get lonely too," Roisin said to me one afternoon, back before Dublin was our home and all we knew was Kerry and school, the country roads we chased every night and the hedge between our houses. "It's why they need a partner in their cage. Without one, they actually get depressed. Isn't that mad?"

All Saturday afternoons last forever when you're seventeen. That one especially though, in our small town outside of Tralee, seemed perpetual.

"That's mad, yeah," I replied. I was sitting next to her on the three-seater sofa in her mother's living room, legs crossed. A maths textbook rested on my lap, one stolen from the pile of books and notepads that littered the marble floors.

The documentary – some nature programme on RTÉ One about parakeets that ebbed and flowed from my concentration – was supposed to be background noise while we studied, but at some point Rosin became engrossed.

"They literally need another bird friend to be happy," she continued, gnawing on the tip of her Bic pen. She did that so often, chewing on the plastic casing until it cracked, that one day, in French class, I turned to see her lips painted blue; it took a week for the ink stains to fully leave her front teeth.

"The mocks are starting in two days, Ro," I said, mostly frustrated at my own lack of preparation. "Unless there's a surprise exam on the complexities of budgies, I think we should get back to this."

Shushing me, Roisin said, "Higher it up there." When I refused, she stole the remote from underneath my leg and increased the volume herself.

"The death of a companion can be harrowing for the parakeet, with many suffering from extreme anxiety in their absence," came the dull voice of the narrator, the shot then cutting to a lone parakeet in a cage.

The neon green bird wailed in sorrow, its cries akin to an agonizing widow's.

"Jesus," I said. "Talk about light viewing before Winning Streak."

Roisin didn't respond, didn't even move. My friend was lost in thought beside me, her eyes wide and glassy as though they'd been scooped out and polished.

She reminded me of a child there, one who'd overheard the truth about where her Christmas presents came from and realized everyone had been lying to her, that life would be full of similar disappointments.

"Ro?" I said, but got nothing. So again, louder, "Roisin?"

She jolted back to life as if defibrillated.

"Promise you won't leave me," she said then.

I knew Roisin worried about the future a lot; the idea of inevitably leaving Kerry was daunting to her. More frightening though was the possibility that our friendship might not survive the move, that it could only exist in a certain time and place. At school. In-between hedges. On country roads.

I shifted on the couch, turned my whole body to her. "Roisin. Come on."

"No, Clare, promise me," she said again, her voice frantic then, as though imagining the very thing. "Everything will be different soon. Everything's changing."

She dropped her head to the floor, began picking at her nails.

I didn't know what to do. Such bold expressions of emotion always made me uncomfortable. Even at my grandfather's funeral I had to pinch myself under my dress to spur tears, because crying with an audience went against all of my instincts.

I put my hand on Roisin's arm, touched it cautiously as if petting a lion.

"Before you know it, you'll be off to Dublin," she said, sniffling. "You'll make lots of new friends at Trinity, the kind of people you've always wanted to be around, and I'm afraid there won't be space for me anymore."

"There'll always be space for you, Ro," I said. "And sure you'll be in Dublin too. We'll be there together."

That assurance didn't work before, and it would not work then either. I had to resort to the only method I knew to persuade her. I let my hand fall from her arm and clenched it into a fist, my pinkie finger jotting out like the spout of a teapot.

She smiled, relief colouring her face again, and curled her finger around my own.

"I promise I won't leave you if you won't leave me."

"I promise," she replied, tightening the grip.

I think about that day a lot now.

five

The honeybee has one good sting in them. After it's spent, they leave so much of their body behind – their nerves and muscles and insides – that the rupture is often fatal; it kills the bee to do the very thing it's known for.

Home again, I found myself at the desk in my room, the laptop screen casting a pale light over my face like the glow from a fish-tank. An hour or two had ticked by already, the space around me sinking into a grey-blue nightmare, and I had nothing but a shallow paragraph to show for it.

I typed on, a horse sauntering from the gate rather than bolting.

New words gradually formed sentences, those sentences building paragraphs, and that's all writing really was.

Construction on solid foundation. But I didn't love what I was writing, grew more and more frustrated with every tap on the keyboard.

There wasn't anything wrong with what I'd written per se, but if you stare at a sentence long enough, it starts to play tricks on you.

I eventually highlighted the entire document, pressed the backspace key.

My work blinked away.

Whatever pool of inspiration I used to drink from had dried up, and I thought then: maybe writers can be like bees too. Maybe, like poor Emily and Sylvia before me, I only ever had one story to tell, one sting to prove myself with, and all that remained for me now was the long wait.

When things were good, I could write anywhere. No room was too small or dark, no coffee shop too loud. Silence wasn't a necessary condition for my output; I didn't need isolation to break into a story. I could do it right in front of you, slip behind that wonderful curtain, and you'd be none the wiser, a thief burgling your home while you slept.

Ta-dah! I was here all along.

Of course, I didn't welcome distraction either, and there were definitely certain constants I thrived under. A comfortable and clean workspace, for instance. Soothing music in the background, strictly classical. A cup of tea, golden brown with just the right amount of sugar. And they were all present there, urging me on.

So why then, when I slipped behind that curtain, was I met only by a concrete wall?

"Are you a writer or something?"

I jolted in my seat, twisted to the door. Zoe was standing there, a silent apparition peeking through the gap like a voyeur. The apartment was so quiet when I returned earlier, like the ghostly corridors of a school at night, that I figured she'd gone out.

How long had she been there for?

"Or something," I replied, glancing to the blank screen. "Are you settling in okay?"

Zoe moved inward with the door, clutching the handle. "Everything's great, thanks," she said, leaning against my wardrobe then. The blonde light from the hallway split my room in half like the ground had shifted apart. "I hope I'm not interrupting though."

I stretched the sleeves of my sweater over my hands. "You're grand, don't worry."

But I was exposed, caught in the shameful act of idleness.

"You look lovely. Where are you off to?"

Zoe had transformed since I saw her this afternoon. If possible, she looked even more attractive, the kind of girl who derived attention from both men and women on the street but in two very different ways.

The dark clothes she wore earlier, tired and crinkled from the fuss of travelling, were swapped for a white and green stripped t-shirt and denim dungarees, one side unbuttoned and flapping down in that effortless, *Fresh Prince* kind of way.

She had make-up on too and her hair, tied up and matted before, now skimmed her shoulders and writhed in soft, loose waves, each strand delicately woven to her scalp by the most gifted of seamstresses.

"Nowhere," she replied as if the thought had never even crossed her mind thank you very much, and I resented her for it, resented her in the same way I did those people who woke up twenty minutes earlier than they needed to just to meditate.

At twenty-eight years old, had I already reached that sticky age where getting dolled up so late in the day meant there had to be some looming special occasion? That doing so anyway, without such an excuse, was just borderline maniacal? I liked to think I hadn't. But then again, I'd recently started to consider brushing my teeth and applying deodorant as dressing up. So really, who was I to talk?

"I was actually just checking if it's all right to use the kitchen?" Zoe said, throwing a thumb behind her. "I know some hosts can be a little weird about that."

"Of course. Work away."

"Great," she said with a twist of her shoulder. "I'll let you get back to it then."

Spinning on her feet, those bare and dainty little things, she left then, closing my door with the delicacy of someone sneaking from an unpleasant one-night stand.

I wanted to follow her at once, to stalk Zoe around my house like a shadow and see what she got up to when I, the omnipresent eyes and ears, wasn't around. She both fascinated and terrified me, the combination dizzying, and I wondered just how much I could trust her in my home.

What did I really know about this woman? I thought.

Sure, a quick glance of her Bunker profile would give me the basics, but I of all people knew how deceptive those things could be. Take my profile, for example: my page boasted a happy, welcoming woman, eager for interaction and culture swapping, and was embellished with photos from a life I no longer lived.

I tapped on my desk over and over until the sound mimicked my heartbeat, wondering what kind of lies Zoe's Bunker profile told.

Curiosity soon got the better of me; exiting out of Microsoft Word, I pulled up the Bunker homepage on my laptop and clicked on the requests icon beside my profile picture, a little symbol of a notepad and pen that reminded me of a better way I could spend my time.

Nonetheless, I scrolled through countless past solicitations; the Canadians who left this morning; the German from last week who walked around in his underwear; the moody Londoner before him who definitely thought I was an agoraphobe. But I couldn't find Zoe's. I must have scanned the list a dozen times, all to no avail.

Think, Clare, I said to myself. Think.

I went to my inbox then, vaguely remembering the brief message Zoe had attached to her booking request like an enticing blurb on the back of a novel. Pick me, pick me, pick me!

My stomach dropped.

The message was there, but Zoe's display photo had vanished, reverting to the ominous mugshot of a faceless, grey entity. Gone too was her username, once blue and clickable, now black and impervious. A dead end. A full stop. Turn back, there's nothing here for you, it said; *user not found.*

Had she really deleted her page?

I vaulted from the chair and to the door, but my hand stalled on the handle.

You can't just go out there, guns blazing, I told myself. You have to be careful, Clare, discreet in your investigation.

See, there's a particular art in extracting information from someone without them ever knowing. It's something I learned from my mam in the way she carried herself around my father, in how she moved and spoke, teasing out parts of him like unsavoury grey hairs. The trick was to be so subtle, so cunning in your performance, that they actually offer themselves up, that they lay their palms flat down to you and say: *Here, read me. Know me.*

Earlier, I would've done anything to distance myself from Zoe, but now I found myself looking for an excuse to be as close to her as possible. The answer was sitting right there on my desk, a miniature *thank-you* card tied to its neck with gold string.

I snatched the bottle of Cabernet Sauvignon the Canadian's, my unwitting enablers, had left for me and strode into the bright hallway, found Zoe fussing about in the kitchen, sliding a frozen pizza into the oven.

"Fancy a glass of wine?" I asked, not quite believing the words as they spilled out. Was I actually that desperate to stray from my work? I mean, what was it to me if Zoe had deleted her page? By morning she'd be gone and I'd never have to think of her again.

Zoe spun away from the oven, surprised to see me untethered from my room.

"I was already planning to give you five stars, but that just sealed the deal."

I smiled, invitation accepted, and came into the kitchen. "Red okay?"

"I'm normally a pinot kind of girl myself. The last time I drank red, I couldn't remember my name the next morning." She giggled, and I wanted to tell her that that was the point, that I'd long stopped drinking wine out of enjoyment.

"If it can't be fixed with a tall glass of wine," I was saying then, retrieving two tumblers from the press above the sink, "then it might never be."

Those were Roisin's words and how adulterous it was to use them with someone else.

I set the pair of glasses down on the narrow breakfast bar, their bases chiming against the black marble, and fetched the corkscrew as Zoe made her way around.

She watched me uncork the bottle then, head in her hands like a child, and cheered when the cork came free with a *pop*, giving way to a rich smell of blackcurrants and dark chocolate, a scent that mingled in the air with the pizzas.

"Say when," I advised her, tilting the bottle above her glass. The dark ruby liquid trickled down the edges like a velvet rain, and I hated how the insides of my mouth came alive, anticipating the taste.

The ornate tumblers were a housewarming gift from Fiona, but they were limited now; mugs weren't the only thing I was inclined to drop, particularly after a glass or two.

Each one contained a star there, sharp and shifting, a trick of light from a sun in descent over the city.

"When!"

She brought the glass closer to her, but waited until I poured one for myself – our *when!* somewhat different – before drinking it. Then, saluting each other, we took our first taste together. At a glance, you wouldn't be crazy to consider us friends then. Housemates, even.

"So, a writer?" Zoe finally said, a finger tracing the rim of the tumbler.

"*Mmm!*" The glass was at my mouth again, my breath steaming up its insides. I didn't know what to say, anyway; I might've been the only writer who didn't like to talk about the fact that they were a writer.

Zoe laughed. "What's it like? Being a writer, I mean."

"Challenging." It was all I could think of that wasn't either rubbing a great job in her face when it was good or admitting that it was soul-draining when it was bad.

However, it wasn't the answer she was expecting and I could see that she didn't know what to do with my response, looking at me as though I'd given her a fork to eat soup with.

"I suppose even the best of jobs can be shite at times."

Sometimes, to say you are a writer, or any kind of artist, is to then feel like you have to spend the next five minutes justifying your admission somehow. And I just wasn't in the mood then. Besides, this was supposed to be my interrogation, not hers.

"And what is it you do in Belfast?" I asked, cocking my head in the way all southerners do when talking about the north, my aim way off and actually hitting the docks and the Irish Sea beyond.

"Piano," Zoe said candidly, and then… what *was* that? A flash of insecurity, almost imperceptible, streaking across her face like a streetlight on the motorway. "Well, I teach most of the time. Kids and teenagers, bored housewives, that kind of thing. But on the weekend I play at a bar in town." She looked down as she spoke, tucked a stray piece of hair behind her ear. "It's nothing special. They don't even pay me yet. But I enjoy it all the same."

I'd forgotten what that's like, I thought to myself. But I must have said it aloud too because Zoe then asked: "Forgotten what, Clare?"

Earlier, back in Fiona's office, I had to face the fact that I'd veered off course and lost sight of my destination. That was a hard pill to swallow, but harder was realizing then that I'd forgotten why I was even pursuing this career in the first place. I'd forgotten that, at one stage, writing wasn't for money or validation or to feel better about actually calling myself a writer to some stranger. I wrote because I loved every minute of it.

I swallowed the contents of my glass. "Nothing."

Later, after peeling away slices of pizza until all that was left were speckles of crumbs on a white plate, a crusty map of the world, Zoe wandered over to the sitting room, nuzzling her glass of wine. During dinner, I managed to sneak a second bottle in and Zoe had smiled like a mischievous villain.

"Is this you?"

I turned away from the sink where I was rinsing the plate, caught her stealing a paperback from the small bookcase behind the sofa. It was my fault for leaving them there, I guess.

"Mm-hmm," I replied, slotting the plate into a niche in the dish rack.

It wasn't me, however, in the same way a baby photo wasn't quite me either. I wrote that book, that is true, I extended my heart first through pen and paper, then onto a keyboard, and pressed it for the world to see, but it was also true that I didn't recognise the person who did that anymore and I'm trying to work out how those opposing ideas can coexist.

I dried my hands and then topped up my glass again, joining Zoe in the living room. She was flipping my book back and forth, pouring over it in amazement.

"I actually think I remember this," she said, looking up to me. She was holding it in both hands then, like Charlie and his golden ticket. "This was like *everywhere*, wasn't it?"

“Everywhere and then nowhere.” She passed me the book, and I turned it over, cringing at the black and white author shot at the bottom.

Where are your siblings, little one? I wondered. Dumped to the bottom shelves? Buried behind flashier covers and more notable names? I pictured my books not in the hands of enthralled readers anymore but as makeshift coasters, collecting brown, sticky rings, or as quirky decorations in some beatnik café. The only function they served now was being the flat surface you need when composing a shopping list or a birthday card.

“You’re going to do another one, right?” Zoe asked.

I considered the question, returning the book to her like a counterfeit banknote. What was once so heavy in my hands now felt weightless, as though I could flip through it and find nothing but blank pages.

“You’ll have to wait and see.”

Zoe nodded and, much to my relief, spared me any follow-up questions. She went back to the stand, replacing my book, and then exclaimed: "Jesus! It's been years since I've seen one of these things."

She crouched down, ogling over an ancient karaoke machine on the bottom shelf. Its silver head was coated with fine dust, its monitor grey as slush. Next to it was a collection of compilation CD's and two dynamic microphones, both coiled in their black cables.

I nearly died the day Roisin hauled the eyesore into the apartment, a relic from the early noughties that just didn't *belong* anymore, like UGG boots and video cassettes.

"What?" she had said with a grin. "I told you I was going to get one, didn't I?"

In fairness, she did tell me. But I thought that was just drunken discourse at the karaoke bar we'd been frequenting. I didn't know then what I know now, that Roisin had a way of finding brief enjoyment from something and obsessed over it until her attention was lured elsewhere. Why would karaoke be any different?

"Yeah, my old housemate, Roisin, was a karaoke enthusiast," I said to Zoe, sitting behind her on the armrest of the sofa. I can't remember the last time I spoke her name out loud, at least to someone else; it felt odd, like calling a parent by their first name.

Zoe stood up straight, wine swooshing in her glass. "Aye, but not you?"

"No, I grew to love it," I admitted, hot from the drink then and more tolerant, more accessible. "We were kind of a big deal at this one place in town actually, even applied for some national competition thing." I laughed then. "Can you believe that? An all-Ireland karaoke contest. I don't know what we were thinking."

She was laughing along with me too. "Why did you stop?"

"Why do we ever stop doing the things we love?" I asked, looking up to Zoe as though she was a god – a god with a nose ring and I, her hesitant zealot. "Too much of a good thing, I suppose."

She plopped down onto the couch, crossed her legs, her bare foot extended and roaming the air as though conducting music I couldn't hear.

"Do you miss it?"

I let my body tumble down from the armrest like a bag of apples, landed on the mushy cushion next to Zoe.

"Sometimes. A lot, actually."

We were side by side then, the closest we'd ever been to each other, and I noticed how much I liked it. There's a particular intimacy in being that close to someone; you see it on idealistic teenagers at the movies, knees bumping, arms pressed together, their skin electric.

"You should go back, Clare."

"I thought about it, but it wouldn't be the same." Just like my apartment, every corner of that bar on South William Street would be haunted, its walls tainted with memories like a rancid mould – memories I felt compelled to share with Zoe then.

I told her about the night Roisin and I were booed off stage for butchering *Total Eclipse Of The Heart* – Zoe wincing with second hand embarrassment for me – and the redemption the following week with our renowned take on

Time After Time, a performance that would make us little legends in Cobblers.

There was also the night we swore we wouldn't sing, both of us dying from a flu that nearly rendered us voiceless. We wound up in the spotlight anyway, of course, croaking along to some Westlife song like Patty and Selma after a tonsillectomy.

"Which was the same night," I added, "that I met a boy named Jack."

Handsome, charismatic Jack Murray, the tallest boy in the bar who bought us drinks all night and then, in the hectic smoking area, leaned into my space and whispered his desire to take me on a date; Jack Murray, whose baggy Sligo jersey I wore the next day at breakfast, the smell of his aftershave all over my body like a rash; Jack Murray, whose lips were both hard and tender on mine, whose acne was even attractive.

Zoe was playing me at my own game, I realized, but I couldn't help it. She made it so easy to talk, the serenity that orbited her latching onto me like a contagion. However, if I knew what she was going to say next, I never would've left my room.

"You have to take me," she said, shooting forward. "We have to go, Clare!"

"Tonight?" You'd swear she just asked me for a spare kidney, a request I'd sooner fulfil than going to Cobblers of a Friday. "Oh, I don't know, Zoe. Look at the state of me, I'm only fit for bed."

Recently, leaving my apartment at all, even for the bare minimum, aroused some apprehension in me, but the thought of going to Cobblers was a different kind of terror, like going to a school reunion when you have no accomplishments or cute children to flaunt.

"Oh, wise up!" she retorted, rising from the couch as if we already decided it. "We'll only go for one sure. You don't even have to sing, if that's what you're worried about."

She offered me her hand then and, with the amber sunlight slanting through the windows behind her, it looked as though it was doused in honey.

I yearned for the old me in that moment; the Clare who couldn't tell the origin of every sound from her apartment building, who didn't eat dinner alone in her bedroom every night and say things like, *I think I've seen this episode of Antiques Roadshow already.*

Was she even there anymore?

"Just one," I conceded, taking Zoe's hand and letting her pull me up.

I told her I needed ten minutes and then dashed to my bedroom, deciding first to discard my stale sweater and jeans for the only things in my wardrobe that didn't need ironing: a grey plaid skirt and a black polo neck top, an outfit I didn't quite have the self-assurance for but wiggled into, anyway.

After changing – holding my body like an awkward teen in a locker room – I found a pair of black Chelsea boots under my bed that hadn't seen the light of day since New Year's Eve and then started on a more pressing matter: my face.

Afraid of overdoing it, I only applied some mascara and lipstick, rummaging through my handbag to retrieve the battered red tube that always gets in the way when searching for my keys or phone.

I tied my hair up too, wispy bangs framing my gaunt face like a Roman helmet, and then scanned myself in the mirror, my body fuming with a clammy heat from all the hassle.

Getting ready in a hurry is never ideal, but I didn't look too bad. I tried to imagine what I looked like from someone else's perspective too, a trick I'd learned to do in my adolescence. It helped me to be less critical of my appearance, to focus on the bigger picture and not the tiny pixels of imperfections that most people didn't even notice.

I brushed my hands along myself, fingers strumming against my bony ribcage, and decided that yes, I looked okay. Or, at least, I looked decent enough to be seen by any familiar faces that would undoubtedly pop up like whack-a-moles at Cobblers.

Maybe the old Clare was gone, I thought, but I could still do my best to impersonate her.

"Well *hello!*" said Zoe, materializing at the door again. "Look at you, Miss See-Me-After-Class. I feel underdressed now." She had a black jacket folded over her arm, one of those fluffy handbags hanging from her shoulder by a silver chain strap.

"Sorry, is it too much?" I asked, and then felt stupid standing there, as though I'd tried way too hard to mimic Zoe's effortless image. "I can change if…"

"Not at all, Clare." She shook her head. "You're gorgeous."

I didn't know where to look, began touching my face as though trying to hide the smile that was twitching in my mouth.

"Are you all set?"

"One second," I said, and then downed the last of my wine in a single gulp.

Zoe looked impressed, nodded like: not bad.

"Okay, let's go."

six

It was nearly nine o'clock by the time we came out onto the quays and, though the air had become crisper since that afternoon, we decided to walk the twenty minutes or so to South William Street.

We crossed the Liffey over the Samuel Beckett Bridge, a striking, white overpass inspired by Ireland's emblem, the Celtic harp. It's string-like cable stays stretched to an arced pylon in the sky where two seagulls squawked and chased each other like childhood sweethearts.

"Are you excited?" Zoe asked me, linking her arm with mine as we traversed the path.

I stiffened from her display of affection but did not stop, suddenly very conscious of every step I took, of how it felt like Zoe was leading me somewhere.

"Nervous," I admitted, looking out over the water. Without the galvanising sun that had bleached it all day, it now looked large and murky, the home of some grimy monster.

We passed a homeless woman perched on the concrete then, a withered paper cup by her feet that had one word scrawled onto its body: *please*.

Respectfully, Zoe waited until we were two steps away from her before speaking again, as though being anything other than silent and guilty, when someone else was so miserable, was a cruel thing to do.

"Nerves are good. Excitement is nothing without them."

We came out onto the south side of the city, started towards Townsend Street.

I was telling Zoe about Samuel Beckett for some reason, about how he had been stabbed by a pimp in Paris and, whilst recovering in hospital, was frequently visited by his tennis acquaintance, Suzanne Something, a French pianist that he'd soon marry.

Zoe seemed both shocked and amused by the writers life and so I pressed on, surprising myself by how much I actually knew about him – you couldn't study English at Trinity without picking up a few facts about its former, more eminent students, I guess – and using that knowledge to dispel any silence that might've bloomed on our journey.

"I liked that story," she told me later as we turned onto Townsend. The street yawned ahead of us and was unusually quiet, like there had been some city-wide evacuation we were too busy drinking wine to hear about.

"Which one?"

"The stabbing one." I think she was drunker than I thought. "It's lovely."

"*Uh*, maybe I'll catch up with you later, Zoe," I said, turning away from her in jest. She half laughed, half choked.

"No, stop. You know that's not what I meant." She pulled me back into stride. "It's just nice because, if that *terrible* thing didn't happen, if he didn't get stabbed, he might never have fallen in love with your one, right? It's like proof that sometimes awful things need to happen to allow room for the good things, you know?"

I licked my teeth, nodded. Was something good on its way to me?

Conversation lulled for a moment and I considered asking Zoe about the whole Bunker mystery, but decided against it; the closer we were getting to town, the less space I had in my mind to think about anything other than Cobblers and how terrified I was of pushing open its green doors again.

Wasn't I safe in my room just an hour or two ago?

A car crept by us then, reminding me that there was still life out there, the faint sound of its stereo throbbing like the indistinct conversations I sometimes heard my neighbours having through the walls.

Zoe made a passing comment about the sombre red-brick houses that reminded her of the ones back in Belfast and then asked if I was okay because I seemed quiet; I didn't think she knew me well enough to know any different.

"I think the wine is hitting me," is what I said, but I'm not sure it convinced her.

We chased the road up to College Green, the three-sided plaza in city centre where streets seemed to spill into one another like a confluence of asphalt rivers.

Everything came to life at that spot, the pavements scattered with commuters, the roads crawling with cars and buses coming from every direction, and it was there that I could see how Dublin City might be confusing to tourists; with no distinct shape or system, you either knew where you were going or Google Maps was your best friend.

The entrance to Trinity was there too, it's unassuming, pillared facade concealing a sprawling oasis beyond. Every time I passed through its arched doorway as a student, I felt like I was being transported to another world, like I'd slipped into a parallel universe wherein which I was exactly who I needed to be.

Some days I missed it. Most days, I forgot I ever went.

"It's just around the corner here," I said, halting at a pedestrian traffic light. A Luas snaked by us, disappeared up to Grafton Street.

We scampered across the road, narrowly dodging a cyclist, and suddenly I became the navigator then. Zoe tugged on my sleeves like we might get separated amongst the throngs of people and only let go again when we finally reached the bar on South William.

"Is this it?" she asked outside Cobblers, sizing up the building.

Wedged between a glossy hair salon and a corner café that sold overpriced, pastel macarons, you wouldn't be wrong to overlook the narrow bar on a quest to find a suitable spot; the shiny red paint on its veneer was cracked in places, peeling off like dry skin, and its many oblong windows were tinted grey, which always made it hard to determine whether it was busy inside or not.

"Not what you were expecting?"

"It's like an old man's pub," Zoe remarked. "I kinda love it though."

In an effort to entice patrons inside, the bars green door was held open by a clump of Guinness beer mats stuffed under its end, a flashy sign fixed above its brass knob that proclaimed: *Karaoke Night! Eight 'til Late!*

Excited, Zoe went in first, melting into the brown innards of the cavernous pub until she became just another dark silhouette amongst the rest. I stole a moment there on the cobble stones before following her, hands in my pockets scratching furiously against the denim.

The room seemed smaller than I remember, though I always thought that about returning to places of significance after a long time away, and it was typically buzzing. Every barrel table was occupied, the ones who weren't lucky enough to have seating just standing about the place, and the bar was swelling with people waiting to order.

I scanned the room for Zoe and spotted a flash of colour in the centre of the room, as though a heavenly spotlight was shining right onto her. Rambling through the crowds towards her, invisible hands pulling me here and there, I kept my head down.

"This place is great!" She had to shout over the noise; we'd interrupted two men on the cramped stage, giving it their all to *Mr. Brightside*. I hated that song, but the audience were loving it, joining in at the chorus. Even Zoe was bobbing her head like one of those dashboard dogs.

We watched them for a moment, panic rising in my throat; I wasn't claustrophobic, but the crowd was overwhelming and there was always someone trying to scoot past or shift into my space.

I can't imagine I ever enjoyed this.

"I'll grab us some drinks," I said over the music. "You try get us a table somewhere. There's usually some space at the back."

Zoe twisted to the back of the room, then held up two thumbs. "Dead on," she said.

It took ten minutes of queuing before I reached the counter, the dapper bartender on the other side asking what I wanted whilst pulling a pint of golden beer for someone else.

"Two glasses of white," I shouted across to him, struggling to even hear myself; a middle aged woman had took to the stage and was midway through a depressing – and slightly concerning – interpretation of *I Will Survive*.

Like he'd only just noticed me then, the bartender looked up from the tap. "Clare?" he said, the skin around his dark eyes creasing as if he was seeing a mirage in a desert. "Jesus, it's been ages."

He passed the foaming pint of Heineken to the lad next to me, saying, "You'd want to watch yourself around this one, man. She's a pickpocket."

The boy, barely eighteen, flung me a disconcerted look and then shot away to his friends.

"Are you trying to get me in trouble, Dan?" I jeered, hating how I sounded when I was trying to be casual, as though it was all just improv.

Smirking to himself, Dan fetched two wine glasses from a rack and freely poured some pinot into them, filling them up way more than he would for anyone else.

"You don't need any help with that." He slid the drinks across the counter to me and waved his hand when I offered him a twenty euro note, like the very idea of it was offensive. "For old times' sake," he said, solemnly. "We've missed you around here. We've missed both of you."

Unable to match his gaze, I turned my cheek to him. "Thank you, Dan," I said, taking the drinks. "Catch up with you later, yeah?"

I left before his parted lips could form another word.

It was exactly what I'd been afraid of; there was no way I could go the night, particularly in Cobblers, without *something* being said. That would be like going to a wedding and getting angry every time there was a toast.

But maybe that was it, I thought, maybe I'd gotten it out of the way and was free to enjoy the reception now.

Zoe managed to find us a table, a cosy nook near the doors to the smoking area. We had to deal with people rushing in and out, the door banging each time, and a slight draft, but it was better than standing. We wouldn't be staying long, anyway.

"Cheers!" said Zoe, clinking her glass against mine.

We were watching the next pair of performers – Zoe mouthing along to the yellow words as they streamed across a projector behind the singers – when my phone throbbed on the table. It was an e-mail from Fiona. *How's the writing going? Spoke to Mister Eggs himself after you left. Expect a call from him tomorrow*, it read.

"Who's Mister Eggs?" Zoe asked, peering at my screen. The bones on her face looked sharp by candlelight, but her skin appeared smooth, like tangerine ice-cream left in the sun too long. I imagined swiping my finger across it, tasting her.

"My publisher, Eamon," I explained, massaging the stem of my glass. I locked my phone, left it face down on the table again. "It's kind of an inside joke."

The first time we ever met, Eamon Browne had peculiarly likened my eldest manuscript and I – it's umbilical cord not quite severed yet – to flour and butter.

"I want you to think of me as the eggs, Clare," he had said in his office on Amiens Street, hands clasped on the desk like a teacher at a parents meeting. "And you can't have a cake without the eggs, can you?"

I told Zoe about his metaphor for success and she scoffed. "What a pig!"

Though he was a reasonable man and I'd never had anything more than a creative quarrel with him, I do remember being startled by what he said to me in his office that day, as though I'd never fully realize my potential without his input. And back then, fresh out of Trinity, nothing scared me more than unrealized potential.

We watched two more performances in silence, and then Zoe stood for the bathroom.

"Be right back," she assured, a bit wobbly, and I picked up my phone again, wanting to appear busy and unapproachable in her absence.

I scrolled through Twitter, retweeting a thread exposing the horrors of Direct Provision in Ireland, and then found myself back on Fiona's message, scouring it for clues like it was a riddle I couldn't solve. *Expect a call from him tomorrow* – I kept rereading those words, wondering if Fiona actually meant to say: Prepare for a call tomorrow.

Was I really in that much trouble?

Drafting a blasé response to her, I was so focused on my screen that I didn't react to my name being announced at first; it sounded so foreign over the speakers, like when you say your name to yourself and it never sounds right or like it belongs to you.

"Clare? Where are you, love?" The scrawny, bald host was on the stage there, sweeping the crowd for me with the flat of his hand over his eyes. I tried to make myself smaller, sinking into my chair, but eventually he spotted me in the corner and beamed into the microphone, "*Ah*, there she is!"

I felt eyes on me everywhere and didn't know what to do with myself, like when a waitress is singing happy birthday to you and you kind of just sit there, motionless. The host beckoned me to him. I shook my head, like: no, but thanks anyway. But then Dan was there at my table, and I ought to have known he had something to do with this.

"Come on, Clare," he said. I glared at him and he just laughed, my discomfort delighting him as though it was all part of some game I was playing. "It's your song and all."

I looked to the screen and saw that *Time After Time* had been queued up, the tune Roisin and I always turned to at two in the morning, when everyone had long lost the ability to judge anything with sense. My mouth watered like when you're about to throw up.

"No, Dan, seriously. I can't," I protested, pulling at the neck of my top like my skin was gasping for air. It would be nothing without her, a desperate revival of something that I only ever had a small part in. But the crowd got behind him then, encouraging me with a tender round of applause.

I felt pressured to do something, to stop the attention no matter the cost; I stood up, almost involuntarily, like God himself had hoisted me, and Dan steered me to the stage like a mannequin. A myriad of condoling faces rolled by me, imprinting on my brain. They'd be on my bedroom ceiling that night, mocking me as I tossed and turned.

At the microphone, I took in a deep, jagged breath, and silence rippled throughout the room. I wanted to melt into the floor like wax, to seep through the cracks and grow again on the other side – an open and deserted place where no one could find me.

The familiar music started, and I glanced to the right, chewing on my thumbnail. Nothing was there but empty space and disappointment, and I realized how alone I was up there, the most alone I'd ever felt, which was an unsettling sensation considering how many people were surrounding me.

I thought of the parakeet from the nature documentary… its tortured wails… the pinkie-promises.

The words to the song appeared on a smaller screen in front of me and I opened my mouth to sing, but nothing came out. The words lodged at the top of my throat as though the chains in my larynx had detached from their rings.

I was wrong; I didn't miss this. I didn't miss this at all.

The lyrics forged ahead without me, the microphone amplifying nothing but my shaky breath. Someone shouted words of encouragement and there were another series of claps, but I couldn't do it. A flash of light at the back of the room – the doors to the smoking area opening – and I was gone.

I let the microphone fall to the floor, its piercing squeals blaring from every speaker around the room, and drove through the crowds until cold air smacked my face.

seven

The smoking area was loud and smelt like a wet ashtray, but there was a lot more space out there. People stood in small groups of two and three, pumping milky clouds from their chests into the night sky like exhaust pipes.

Finding a spot away from them in the corner, I fell flat against a stone wall, pulling sharp breaths into my lungs like I was in labour. A mounted heater hummed above me, periodically ticking on and off like I was never even there, and drenched me in a warm, orange glow.

Was I more angry or humiliated? I didn't know. The two feelings raged inside of me like tornados butting against one another. I tried swallowing them, but somehow the acknowledgment of their existence only seemed to make them more potent, like a hole getting bigger the more you took away from it.

I could've screamed but remained completely still, a tower collapsing upon itself in total silence. Two girls beside me flicked ash onto the concrete, their shoulders shaking with laughter, and I wanted to claw at them for being so insensitive; their ignorance to my pain felt like a direct attack, but how could they know?

"Clare?" When I heard my name again it didn't sound alien to me, but familiar and full of colour, like I'd chosen it myself. But that was mostly owing to the person speaking it; Jack Murray always sounded as though his voice had been passed through a sieve first, removed of any impurities. "Clare, are you alright?"

My ex-boyfriend stood in front of me, hands in his jean pockets, eyes brown like spent matches. I wanted to throw my arms up like: you've got to be kidding me! But I just said, "I thought you moved back home?"

He looked a bit offended by that, his lips becoming a thin line. I noticed that he'd let his stubble come through, probably because he didn't have someone telling him he looked better without it.

"I did," he said. "I'm just down for the weekend." He tossed his head over his right shoulder then, signalling to a blonde girl in a red playsuit behind him. She had a waist like a twelve-year-old and Jack's coat draped over her like a royal mantle. I knew this because it was the coat I'd bought him for Christmas one year.

"Oh right. Lovely."

The girl came forward and Jack introduced us like she was his illegitimate child, touching her hipbone lightly.

Her name was Aoife, a hairdresser from Dublin who had a thick accent and called me *hun* twice, like I was one of her clients from the salon. She looked like the kind of girl who thought she was unique but had a *Live, Laugh, Love* tattoo and often voiced her desire for a Straight Pride, the kind of girl Roisin would mock during one of her impassioned rants.

Jack described me as an old friend from college and then we were all silent for several seconds, as though the understatement was obvious and almost amusing. I did snort a little.

“Do you think we could talk for a minute, Clare?” he asked then.

I nodded buoyantly, like I could go either way about it. And I definitely could have.

Turning to Aoife, Jack said he’d join her back inside in a minute. She wasn’t impressed at all and stared at him as if trying to communicate her outrage telepathically. He didn’t budge though and, before she left, she kissed him hard on the lips, which I thought was more for my benefit than his.

Was I the crazy ex? I wondered. The one he referenced during their pillow talks?

Aoife said goodbye, and I smiled at her without showing my teeth.

“She seems nice,” I said to Jack a moment later. He had joined me against the wall, lit a menthol cigarette. “Where did you find this one? The Zara changing rooms?”

"Don't be like that," he replied, though I knew it was something he would've laughed at before. "It doesn't suit you to be cruel, Clare."

I apologised like I'd just stubbed his toe and then asked how things were going up in Sligo. He said they were good, great actually, his voice quickening as he spoke about the new job he was starting in September, the apartment in Sligo town he'd just moved into.

I tried to appear optimistic for him, but I couldn't help coming across as cold and simulated, as though hearing of his progression only reminded me of how my life had come to a depressing standstill. And then there was the disturbing feeling in the pit of my stomach that I'd actually been holding him back all this time, that if I never ended things with him, he'd still be miserable with me, the crazy ex who anchored him to Dublin.

Maybe Zoe was right before; maybe the awful does make way for the good.

"And what about yourself? How's the book coming along?" It surprised me that he still cared enough to ask about that, even after the torment I put him through. Could this man, probably the last person alive that I knew in each of my senses, still care for me?

Click. Copy. Paste. “It’s good, yeah. I’m almost finished.” But he didn’t buy it, his dark brows sloping over his eyes into a frown like: come on now, Clare. I caught his gaze for a split second and was transported back to the night we first met, standing in that very spot. It frightened me how distant we were from those people then.

He adjusted the watch on his wrist, scratched at an imaginary itch on his cheek.

“Why haven’t you answered any of my texts, Clare?” Jack asked, like he had rehearsed the question a hundred times in his bathroom mirror.

That was the thing about Jack Murray; he was always so direct with his emotions, always wanting to talk things through like mature adults. It was a trait that had set him apart from all the other impassive boys I’d dated. However, as the years went by, it grew irritating, like everything I said or did was intrinsically linked to my feelings for him; I could fall asleep without saying goodnight to him, and the next morning we'd need to have a 'serious talk.'

You could tell he didn't come from a broken home.

"I don't know, Jack. I was busy." The conviction was pitiful, even for me. "And I've been having a bit of shit time lately, in case you'd forgotten."

"That's not fair," Jack insisted, like everything in life fell into two categories: fair and unfair. "She was my friend too, you know. It hasn't been easy on any of us." He left the wall and stood in front of me, and I got the feeling that he was bracing to leave already.

Behind him, the door to the smoking area burst open again, and out spilled a mob of rowdy lads, crooning with their deep, gruff voices. Zoe wandered out after them looking a bit lost, my bag and jacket in her hands, and I felt terrible that I'd somewhat forgotten about her. She spotted me in the corner and started towards me, but then saw Jack and thought better of it, perhaps sensing the air of confrontation.

She waited by the doors for us to finish our conversation.

"At some point, Clare, you've got to move on with your life," Jack continued.

"Some of us are better at that than others, it appears." I crossed my arms, lowering my head toward the door, to the girl that waited on him inside, as if challenging him, and I felt rotten for it. He didn't deserve that at all. And I knew I'd revisit that remark later, twisting my words like a Rubik's Cube to make sense of their callousness.

Jack looked at me in an awful way, like: who even are you? And I thought of the last time we'd slept together, of how I didn't make a sound when he finished but just lay there, staring at the ceiling which had left him feeling as though he'd subjected me to something unpleasant, like watery coffee.

He was done with this conversation, I could tell then.

"Good luck, Clare. Take care of yourself." He turned and walked away, shaking his head like I'd said something vulgar.

"Do you not think it would be easier for us to be the kind of exes that hated each other, Jack?" I shouted out to him. He stopped and turned back to me, unbothered by the small audience we'd earned. "At least then you wouldn't have to care at all."

Jack mulled that over like he was taste-testing a wine. His cigarette was all but burned out, belching the last of its life in-between his fingers. And I thought how ludicrous it was that our relationship, once so whole and significant, had reduced to flitting interactions that lasted less than the time it took to have a smoke.

"I could never hate you, Clare," he said solemnly, flicking the cigarette butt to the ground, its embers crashing like tiny meteorites. "I do pity you though. Grieving's awful enough without having to do it alone." He left it at that and I watched him disappear through the door, back into Cobblers.

Immediately, I wanted to run after him, to pull him back by his shoulder and beg him to say sorry and talk to me the way he used to, the way he talks with her now. There's a part of me, weakened from his absence but still very much alive, that will always respond to Jack Murray, like the moon with the tide, and I think it will always be that way. But I was immobilised then, an unimpressive wax figure in the corner of the smoking area.

I thought for a second I might cry. Like, really cry. No pinching required. There was something in Jack's words that penetrated me all over, a cutting truth that I'd been ignoring for far too long; by shutting everyone out, I had undoubtedly made things harder for myself.

Eyes pregnant with tears, I let my head fall against the stone wall.

The sky that night was inky black and stubborn, as if the world was holding a vast mirror up to me, and I found no solace in its emptiness, only an infinite space to project my feelings upon, like a blank page in a notebook.

A lone seagull cut across the black, its white body like a shooting star, and then Zoe appeared in front of me.

Her eyes bounced up and down erratically, as though she was a first responder searching for injuries, and then she put her hands on my arms. I prayed in that moment she wouldn't ask if I was okay because that would surely be my undoing and the crying might never stop.

"What can I do for you, Clare?" she asked earnestly. "How can I help?"

Her tenderness caught me off guard, her voice so soothing I wanted to step into it like a warm bath and let it absorb me, or perhaps suffocate me. I didn't know how to counter it at all, began picking at the cut on my palm, distracting one pain with another.

Was there anything she could do for me, I thought, even if I had the courage to let her? I was a lost cause, like Zoe had found me squashed between a car and a tree, and the only thing keeping me alive was the pressure from both sides; eventually I'd have to come free, I knew that, but for now I was comfortable there.

I reigned in the tears, blinked them away.

"You can buy me a shot," I said with a crooked smile. It was the only thing I could think of, the only remedy for this migraine of a night. What better way to forget my troubles than to chase them away with alcohol?

Zoe smiled, took my hand in hers. "I can definitely help with that!"

She towed me from the smoking area and back into the main lounge. We went straight to the bar inside, Zoe elbowing her way to the counter, and Dan was there again. He started apologizing for earlier, saying how stupid and inconsiderate he felt, his face drooping with remorse like a bloodhound's, but I just cut across him and ordered two tequilas.

I didn't want to talk about it anymore. I just wanted to drink and forget. And I know they have a name for that, but at least I knew it worked. And then, tomorrow, Jack's confrontation and the karaoke catastrophe, maybe even Zoe herself, would all be hazy and somewhat indiscernible from reality.

Dan prepared the drinks without another word and passed us a salt shaker and a lime wedge to lessen the impending burn. He took the money – no fuss this time – and then, at the bar, we licked the salt from the back of our hands and downed the shots simultaneously, sucking on the wedge afterwards like new-born's with their thumbs.

Zoe's mouth puckered from the bitterness and she slammed the shot glass down onto the counter, saying, "Another?"

We repeated this process until our breaths could've been set on fire, until the world and everyone in it seemed to move faster. I was even laughing by then.

After the last shot, Zoe was saying something to me, but I couldn't make sense of her; it was loud in the bar and her words were coming faster than her lips were moving, like the sound on one of those dodgy, pirated movies my dad used to bring home sometimes.

"Dance, Clare! I said we should dance!"

I nodded like it was indisputable; we just *had* to dance.

The karaoke had adjourned for a little while and they were just playing music then, some throbbing, electro pop song by that broody New Zealander.

With no designated dancefloor in Cobblers, you kind of just danced wherever you could find the space, which was usually quite difficult on the weekend. However, Zoe was good at burrowing her way into places and found a small clearing for us opposite the stage.

She leaned into my ear there and asked, "Is here okay?"

"Here's perfect!"

It took me a minute to find my feet though, like a mermaid with brand new legs who has to work on breaking them in first. Zoe got straight into it, however, possessed by the euphoric chorus of the song, and came to life, limb by willowy limb.

"I fucking love this song!" she exclaimed, throwing her head from side to side as if trying to ward off a stubborn wasp, her hair masking her face like the vines across my parents' country house. I felt compelled to watch her like that for ages, jealous of how confident she was in all her movements and also intimidated by every single one of them.

What are you thinking, Clare? I thought. You could never be like that.

I stumbled backwards and knocked into the person behind me.

The jolt nearly sent a pint over his clinically white shirt and he shot me a disgruntled look, like I'd actually clipped the back of his car when he was already running late for work. I apologised way too much, my hands all over the place like Bob Fosse, and then came closer to Zoe, who just laughed at the whole thing and continued dancing in her own world.

Just let me be like that, I thought again. Even for the night. Even for the song.

Even for the time it took to smoke a menthol cigarette.

"Come on, Clare!" Zoe encouraged, noticing my stiffness. The space between us was shrinking, or else I was swelling; I imagined myself like a pufferfish, expanding from stress and becoming this conspicuous monstrosity in the centre of the room.

Stupidly, I told myself that I was too old to dance as well, that, at twenty-eight years old on a Friday night, I should be at home, watching *Murder, She Wrote* reruns whilst crocheting. But then I felt the tequila kicking in, tuning my insecurities like an old radio until all their frequencies ran clear, and I said, "Do you know what? Fuck it!"

I let my hair down then – figuratively and literally – and Zoe cheered.

The music worked its way around my shoulders, creeping down to my hips like a teenager sneaking out at midnight, and I felt myself begin to slacken, as if someone had taken a wrench to all the nuts and bolts in my joints.

And just like that, I was dancing like I didn't know how to stand still anymore.

"The actual state of us, Zoe," I said, shimmying back and forth with Zoe in an ironic yet shameful kind of way. "We look like two eejits!" But she didn't care, and that gave me permission to not care either. And really, what's better than that feeling?

It was a perfect moment, so lucid in its simplicity, its spontaneity. And of course I knew that moment could never last, that it would be like trying to hold on to water and, at best, was just a distraction, but I pretended it could, anyway.

"You're a natural!" Zoe commended, her pink hair bumping about her shoulders.

She took my hand and twirled me around clumsily – I was a foot or so taller than her – and then pulled me into her chest until our noses kissed and I felt the warmth of her breath on my cheeks, like when you step off a plane into a hot country.

We both giggled, then separated again.

"I've missed this," I said. I'd started doing little bounces, the music pulsing from the floor right up to my knees, my arms in the air like contorting branches. "Me and Roisin used to dance all the time."

Zoe was bouncing then too and, under the green lights, the thin layer of sweat on her skin was glimmering, like her very aura was trying to shine through.

"What happened to her, Clare?" she coolly asked. And I loved the way my name sounded in that northern accent, like: *Clur*. "What happened to Roisin?"

It spilled out before I could stop it, like holding a bottle of water upside down.

"She killed herself," I said, so impassively I might've said: Oh, she just nipped to the shops. I was still dancing, still half listening to the song. "Jumped right in front of a train on New Year's Day."

Zoe had stopped moving altogether. She looked very lost and morose suddenly, like a balloon the day after a birthday party, and didn't say a thing, her mouth slightly agape as though waiting for someone else to stuff it with words.

"I know," I said. "Pretty grim resolution, right?"

She shook her head. "Clare, I… I'm so sorry."

I could've told her everything then, the whole thing about Roisin and the signs of existential distress she didn't show or the unanswerable note she never bothered to leave, or how I've been renting her room out on Bunker for months now to fill the black hole she created the minute she leapt off that platform, but that might all be boring and pointless to Zoe, like telling her about a dream I had the night before. So I just shrugged as if to say: what can you do? It is what it is.

The truth is that I'm not really sure I knew anything about Ro's state of mind; even our friendship, in all its might and marvel, seemed to have special privileges that I, or anyone else, were entitled to. Roisin's actions on New Year's Day were so shocking, so senseless, that they were almost arbitrary to everyone, like it just *had* to have been some kind of accident or misunderstanding.

I was doing the delph when Jack Murray called with the news, and, *Yeah right*, was my response. Can you believe that?

It took me a long time to realize that my best friend had hidden, faulty parts, like the O-rings on that ill-fated *Challenger* shuttle, and that she was just so utterly done with the strain of being a living thing that she saw no other option but to escape that suffering in the most irrevocable, horrifying way.

A note definitely would've been nice though. Even Sylvia Plath left a note.

"I don't know what to say," Zoe said mournfully.

"You don't have to say anything. Just keep dancing."

But she couldn't, and I was foolish to think that anything would be the same after telling Zoe the truth about Roisin.

The atmosphere in the room had shifted – I'd forced it to – the music receding away like a morning fog. For a long time it felt as though I was plunging from a very tall building, trying to suck thin air into my lungs, and everything around me grew blurry, the walls and people stretching like they were part of the mirrors in a fun house.

I hadn't just acknowledged the elephant in the room, I'd picked it up and said: look, here it is! Now can we get on with our night please? And there's no coming back from something like that, not really.

Like Roisin, I'd made a permanent decision, but unfortunately I had to stick around to deal with the consequences.

I stopped dancing too and quickly became nauseous, the combination of alcohol settling in my stomach, gurgling like a heavy, toxic waste.

"Clare?" Zoe said. "Is everything okay?" But she was so far away and spinning. I couldn't focus on her at all; the more I tried, the worse I felt.

I could feel myself blanching.

"I think I'm going to be sick," I said, my voice sounding way too big and loud, as though it was trapped within my body.

My tongue teemed with saliva or bile, the nausea reaching up from my stomach and into my throat like a fat arm. I was a bullet through the crowd then, Zoe trailing behind me.

As soon as the fresh air met my mouth, it was irrepressible; I buckled to the cobblestones outside the pub like I'd lost my skeleton and expelled the pungent contents of my stomach onto the ground, my shaky hands and knees pressing hard on the cold granite.

"Oh God! Oh Jesus!" Zoe was saying somewhere around me, but I couldn't tell where; I was seeing stars, my stomach contracting as it prepared to force everything up and out again. "I'll get you some water. I'll be right back."

I always cried when I threw up. Even when daily purging was a conscious decision as a teen – a foul but voluntary act belonging to a then indistinct eating disorder – I cried. And I was crying there too, whimpering and vomiting until I could only heave because there was nothing left to go.

When Zoe returned, I was sitting up against my heels, studying the mess I'd made on the street like a jigsaw puzzle. She passed me a pint of ice cold water, but I could only manage a sip or two from it; the stench of the vomit was filing my nostrils, and I felt ashamed. Mortified. Which, admittedly, was easier to stomach than the queasiness.

I wiped my mouth, put a hand to my forehead. It was glossy and hot, like holding onto a mug of steaming coffee.

A few moments later, Zoe crouched down beside me. She wrapped her arm around my shoulder, the sibling I never had, and said, "Feel better now?"

The glass trembled in my hands and I was weak, but the worst was definitely over.

I twisted to face Zoe, who looked very concerned but also like she might laugh. It was as though she'd never witnessed anyone be sick before and didn't know whether it was a terrible thing, or a funny thing, or a terribly funny thing. But I guess all that depends on the circumstances.

"I'm so sorry you had to see that," I sniffled, the words catching in my battered throat and coming out all mangled. Now that the nausea had passed, all I could feel was bristling humiliation. "I'm not normally like this. It's just been…"

"You don't have to explain, Clare. It happens to the best of us."

But I did have to explain. Honestly, at that stage, I think I even wanted to.

If I was going to be this close with Zoe, or with anybody ever again, I had to surrender a little. As much as I hated it, Jack was right in the smoking area; I couldn't do this alone anymore. It's too exhausting.

"I'm just so angry, Zoe," I admitted, fresh tears sloshing in my eyes. I wiped them away as quick as they'd fallen. "I'm just so angry. All the time."

My words spilled into the air, snagging on a brisk breeze that carried them away down the street. Zoe sat quietly for what felt like forever and I thought then that I might've made a terrible error, completely miscalculating our relationship.

The weight on my shoulder hadn't slackened either but definitely dislodged a little, the first crack in a demolishment that would take more time and a lot more patience.

"Right," said Zoe, slapping her leg. She got back to her feet and offered me her hand then. "Come with me. I've got an idea."

I took it with no hesitation and let her pull me up.

I think I would've followed her anywhere.

eight

"What are you looking for?"

We were halfway up Fade Street, the rustic avenue in town reminiscent of a cosy living room, when Zoe came to a stop and withdrew her phone. She swiped on the screen impatiently, chewing on her bottom lip, and looked up and down from its white glow as if trying to gauge our location.

It was the first time I saw Zoe on her phone, I realized then. I almost considered that she didn't have one, wondered how someone so young and attractive could go the whole day without receiving a single call or text.

Does no one count on her? I thought. Is she never urgently needed?

"A shop just," she said. "There has to be one around here."

She pinched at the map on her screen, unaware that she was in the way of two surly delivery men lugging crates of beer into the French restaurant beside us, its blackboard menus advertising a new cocktail called *The Moulin Rouge!*

"There's a Spar around the corner," I told her. "Come on."

At the top of the road, we turned right on to George's Street and scurried across to the other side, even though the pedestrian lights had just switched back to red and there was an oncoming taxi.

I'm not sure why – I still didn't know where Zoe was ultimately taking me – but we moved as if we were running out of time for something, bolting along the congested pavements until we came upon The George.

It was Dublin's eminent gay bar, which I think was more or less by default at this stage; there wasn't many of them left in the capital. Rainbow flags sprouted from the buildings dark exterior, promising a safe space for the city's more colourful individuals, who fenced the venue in an ever growing queue.

I'd only ever spent a handful of nights there, but Roisin adored the place. Even when we'd return to Kerry on the weekends to visit our parents, she'd often turn to me on the bus and say, "*Raaaging* that I'm missing The George tonight!" And I think it would've been like that no matter where she was in the world, like missing your own bed while on vacation.

I still smile when I look back on the time the host – a glittering drag queen with an outlandish name I can't recall – selected Roisin and three others from the crowd to take part in a dance-off.

Based on audience reaction, she'd made it to the final but eventually lost against her handsome opponent, a well-groomed man who'd discarded his shirt just before the song ended, much to the delight of the arbitrators.

"It's rigged!" Roisin insisted in the glossy bathroom afterwards, pacing along the stalls. "I could've swung from the ceiling like *Pink* and the gays still would've picked your man with the abs."

I laughed in front of the mirror, assuring her I thought she was brilliant anyway, and caught her smiling in the reflection then, like that was all that mattered in the end.

How was that the same girl that threw herself in front of a train?

"It's just up there," I told Zoe, pointing to the twenty-four-hour corner store ahead.

At the Spar – famously dubbed *Gay Spar* because of its proximity to The George – Zoe told me to wait outside. When she came back out two minutes later, she had nothing in her hands, though something lumpy and square bulged in her fluffy handbag.

"What's that?" I asked, gesturing to the mass, but she just tightened her lips and looked at me slyly, like: you'll find out soon enough, don't you worry.

Zoe ambled to the edge of the pavement, glanced around Dame Street. You could see as far down as College Green from that point, a long road reinforced with more bars and restaurants and the kind of shops that only American tourists went into, convinced they'd happened upon a cornucopia of Irish culture.

I wondered how it all looked through her foreign eyes, if the city was just as captivating for Zoe as it once was for me.

Before I moved up for college, my painfully country father warned me that meeting Dublin for the first time would be like meeting someone famous; you build them up to be this remarkable, celestial being who breathes a different kind of air, but find that they are just as ordinary as anyone else.

I was glad to discover that this wasn't entirely true, that any disappointment in the city would have to grow on me like dirty fingernails. And it did; with every Dublin Bus that failed to show or with every hotel that popped up in place of something actually worthwhile, I became more and more disenchanted.

So naturally, I bought an apartment here.

I joined Zoe on the curb then, but she did not cross the street with everybody else. Instead, she threw a hand out in front of her there, flapping it all over the place until she caught the attention of an approaching rickshaw.

It's captain, a young Brazilian man in black shorts and a puffer jacket, steered the two-wheeled, hooded cart towards us, and crudely parked alongside the pavement.

He looked delighted to have finally scored a fare.

"Hop in," he said, his voice smoother than his masculine features suggested, and Zoe climbed inside without a second's hesitation.

"Come on, Clare," she called from the cart, noticing my delay.

"Where are we going, Zoe?"

Zoe groaned theatrically, though not in a way that was meant to unsettle me. It was more of a playful, impatient sound, like when you're trying to convince someone to go out, but they're already in their pyjamas.

A driver caught behind the rickshaw honked their horn twice and Zoe leaned across the cart then, poking her head out between the frames.

"Do you trust me?" she asked, but with the traffic lights on her, painting her face an alarming red, like something straight out of a Stephen King movie, I'm not sure that I did.

After just one night together, it would be naïve to think that I could trust Zoe wholeheartedly. And yet, conscious of seeming meek or unadventurous to her, I nodded anyway, my tongue pressed to the roof of my mouth.

"Then get in," she said, and I did. I gave in because I wasn't ready to go home, because I was probably still a little drunk and because that's what the old Clare would have done. And with just a minor adjustment, one degree of difference, she might still be accessible.

Once inside, squashed next to Zoe on the hard-plastic seat, the driver twisted back to us and asked where we were going.

Zoe hunched forward, said something into his ear that I couldn't discern over the noise of the traffic, and then we took off onto Dame Street, the city soon streaking past me like slides on a PowerPoint, but not sticking.

We sailed by Trinity College again and onto Westmoreland Street, Zoe hanging out of her side like a dog, taking it all in. I was on the other end, however, wishing the whole thing could just end already, trying not to focus on the flurry of buildings and cars and people, all of which seemed to tighten the knot in my stomach.

On O'Connell bridge, the wide, stone link between the north and south sides of the city, with its black, Parisian style lampposts and sandstone balustrades, Zoe caught her first, unobstructed view of the pin-like Spire.

"What does it mean?" she asked, peering upwards. The tip of the steel beacon broke above the roofline of the city and was illuminated from within, the rest of its body gently lit by the street scape below.

It told her I wasn't sure, that the monument didn't really have any cultural connection to the city, but served as a great meeting point or compass, nonetheless. Also, I added, it looked pretty cool when they turned it blue for the latest *Star Wars* movie.

From O'Connell Street, we turned right then, and, after another five minutes of riding into the north side, the driver finally slowed down and said, "Here good?"

"Aye, thanks very much," said Zoe, ushering me out of the cart again.

She didn't have any euros to give him though, so I passed him a battered tenner note and told him to keep whatever was left over, which seemed to both shock and please him at the same time. I felt bad because, for a fee that didn't nearly match his labour, he'd wound up bringing us to a place that we could've easily walked to.

Close to eleven by then, Amiens Street was ominously quiet, save for a few city stragglers migrating towards the bright lights of Connolly Station.

"Why did you bring me here, Zoe?" I asked, the rickshaw driver saluting us on the pavement as he disappeared around the corner, the darkness gradually swallowing him.

"Well, I did some snooping," she said. "That's your publisher's office, right?"

Across the street was the Georgian building that housed Neptune Press, the independent, Irish-owned publisher that produced my first book. Though similar in size and style to Fiona's across town, it was a distinctly less pretty building, joint by an apartment block and a solicitor's office, a black drain pipe running along its paling, red bricks.

Even the flowers on its white windowsills were morose, weeping over their containers with heavy heads.

"Yeah. And?"

"I was thinking about what you said before, back at the bar." She was fussing with her handbag then, tearing at the stubborn zipper. "And something about that Professor Eggs, or whatever you call him, didn't sit right with me. So I thought…"

At that, she got the zipper going and eased out the curious lump from her bag, revealing a six-pack of free-range eggs, its cardboard carton the colour of scorched sand.

It took a moment to click, but when it did…

"So, what? You're going to egg his office?"

"No, don't be silly," Zoe gushed. "*You're* going to egg his office."

She opened the carton and held the eggs out to me, presenting them like a tempting box of chocolates. Baffled, I looked down at the little nest, the red markings on their fragile, burnished bodies like cheap tattoos, and then back up to Zoe. She had this megawatt grin on her face, like it was the best idea she'd ever had, and that made me laugh through my nose.

"You can't be serious," I told her, shaking my head. "I'm twenty-eight years old, Zoe. I'm not egging anyone's property." I knocked the lid shut and Zoe groaned again, except this time she really was frustrated.

"Oh, come on, Clare!" she pleaded. "You said you were angry. What better way to express that anger than with some good old-fashioned vandalism?"

"He's my boss. I could lose my job over something like this!"

"It's an egg, Clare. Wise up," Zoe snickered, her impassivity astounding. "And unless he's going to run forensics on it in the morning, I think you'll be all right."

I let the idea creep into my mind for just a second, imagined the weight of the egg in my hand, how easy it would be to launch it like a grenade, how this simple act of destruction might be, if nothing else, fun to do. But the risk of personal and professional mortification if Eamon ever found out quickly superseded all that.

"No, I don't like this," I said. "I'm going home."

"Suit yourself."

I turned away from Zoe, crossing my arms, but I barely made it three steps before I heard the first egg splatting against Eamon Browne's office window.

Aghast, I spun back around at once.

"Zoe! What are you doing?" I hissed. The gooey innards of the shell were bleeding down the panes, dripping yellow onto the ground.

"What?" she asked, poised with another egg in her fist. "You think you're the only angry person in the world,

Clare?" She wound her arm back like a catapult then and I watched the second egg traverse the street, pulverising against the bricks.

I'd never thought of Zoe as anything other than the kind of person who wasn't obstructed by some unseen pain or misery, the kind of person who belonged everywhere. That was a sucker punch right to my gut, hitting me so hard and unexpectedly that I'm not sure how I kept my balance afterwards.

I tried to picture her sad or crying, or just not smiling all the damn time, but I couldn't. It was an unnatural thing, like a cat barking or an ignorant Lush employee.

"Zoe, I..." but I didn't have words to finish that sentence, regretted ever starting it.

There was a protracted silence between us then, so sustained that I could hear someone in the distance shout, *Mikey, we're gonna miss the fuggin' train!*

"Don't worry about it," Zoe eventually said. "Just go home."

She sounded defeated and didn't look at me when speaking, which made me feel monstrous, like when I silenced an incoming call from my mother the day before and just stared at my screen until it rang out.

I hated this, hated that Zoe was becoming demagnetized to me in some way, and all I could do was stand there like a guilty child, counting all the ways in which I had been the high heat that caused it.

There was no way I was going to leave her then, not if there was still a chance I could salvage things, not when she had been the one reprieve in this nightmare, the safety net catching my falling body. And so, knowing that I'd probably regret it in the morning, I came towards her again and stole an egg for myself.

"Aim for the door," I instructed her. "He's quite fond of his large door."

Zoe bit the edge of her smile, younger looking beneath the garish streetlights there, and then said, "Has he heard of Doctor Freud? I think he'd enjoy his work." And just like that, I felt myself coming back to her, like she'd thrown me a life-ring.

We fired our eggs at the same time. Hard, but not so hard that we'd cause any real damage. This wasn't an exercise in destruction, I realized. It was actually the opposite. And how we howled with laughter when the tiny missiles met the imposing, black door.

"See!" said Zoe, glaring at me like: I told you so. "There's method to my madness."

And I had to give it to her – there was. With every egg that left my hand, I felt something go with it, something that I thought was part of me now, like a new limb.

We stalled when a car approached us, doing our best to appear unsuspicious, but after it passed, Zoe fingered the last egg from the tray and handed it to me, told me to make it count.

I threw it with a grunt; it landed against one of the flower pots, the impact knocking the pot out of place and sending it to the ground, soil spilling out onto the steps.

"Nice one!" Zoe beamed, but at that moment, light burst from the third-floor windows and her joy quickly turned to horror.

There was Eamon Browne, distinguishable even from across the street with his square, static beard and navy sweater vest, probably working late and wondering what all the ruckus was about.

"Oh, shite!" Zoe exclaimed, turning to me, though really she seemed entertained by the prospect of getting caught, her eyes giant like golf balls.

Eamon heaved the window up and shouted something loud and threatening down to the street, but all he would have seen were two curious figures running off into the darkness, their shrieking laughter muffled by the sound of an overground DART rattling by.

We found refuge in a barren Connolly Station, chasing our breaths up the frozen escalator. It worked out well because Zoe wanted to catch her breath and I had been needing to pee since Cobblers.

I left her next to the turnstiles in the fluorescent station hall and didn't fully sit down when I used the toilet, instead choosing to squat awkwardly over the seat like I was afraid of being snatched down the drain.

The bathrooms in Connolly weren't about to win any sanitation awards, not with their persistent smell of urine and sticky floors, but that was something I always did in public restrooms, regardless of their cleanliness.

When I was a child, my mother used to spend five minutes applying sheets of toilet paper to a seat before letting me use it, and I guess that just kind of stays with you, like the irrational fear of quicksand or The Bermuda Triangle.

When I came back out, my hands still damp because the dryer was out of order, Zoe was nowhere to be found.

I looked around, bewildered.

Six of the seven mounted timetables were blank, displaying nothing but an amber message that read, *Welcome to Connolly Station,* which either meant you were here too early or too late. The other proclaimed that the last train of the night was leaving in fifteen minutes, the 11:47 commuter to Dundalk.

I could hear its engine in the distance, humming from platform three.

Faint music came from unseen speakers above, the words of the song indistinguishable from whispers in a church. And, save for an operator in an orange hi-vis, comatose at the barriers, and a gallant pigeon roaming the floor, there wasn't a sinner in the hall.

When I turned on the spot, searching for Zoe, the heels of my boots clacked against the tiles and the sound filled the room.

It was like I'd wandered into a crime scene before the crime actually happened, the backdrop of some cheap re-enactment on *Forensic Files*, and I filled with panic. I wasn't an overtly vigilant person but, for obvious reasons, train stations aroused my anxiety. And there was also the undeniable dread of being a woman in a desolate place at night.

I started to call out Zoe's name, but then there was a sound, melodious and foreign to my bleak surroundings.

There was an upright piano by the ticket machines, a colourful thing with psychedelic illustrations all around its body. They had appeared in several stations around the city in the last few years and quickly became the subject of many viral videos on YouTube and Facebook. Though, I'd never actually seen anyone play on one before.

Zoe was there at the piano, slouched above the keyboard, her fingers moving softly across it. She looked lost as she played, her hair drooping around her face like curtains, and I wondered then if the instrument called out to her, longing for her attention in the same way a pen and paper, or the keys on a laptop, used to yearn for me.

I moseyed towards her, as though afraid of interrupting something so beautiful and intimate, and when she noticed me standing there, an intruder in one of her dreams, she let the notes sink to the ground like snowflakes.

Tentatively, and in the same way she did earlier when discussing her work, as if she was ashamed of her indisputable talent, she tucked a piece of pink hair behind her ear and said, “Sorry, I couldn’t help myself.”

I scolded her for apologizing, because I knew what that was like, to be better at something than someone and feel you have to be remorseful about that.

Roisin sometimes wrote poems that were never accepted at the magazines or websites she submitted them to and, when my first book came out, I could see a sourness in her grey eyes, which led me to believe that, beneath all of her exterior elation, she kind of hated me a little.

I never called her out on it though. Two weeks later, she gave up on the poetry.

“What song were you playing?” I asked. It sounded familiar and was tormenting me like that one actor in a movie you can’t place.

Zoe shifted on the cushioned seat. “Oh,” she said, “ever since you told me that story earlier, I’ve had Cyndi Lauper stuck in my head. Turns out, it’s actually pretty easy to play.”

It was quiet for a moment. The pigeon wandered around us, then shuddered its wings and flew away, landing on top of a shuttered coffee stand.

"Can you play it again?" I asked, swallowing hard. "If you don't mind."

Zoe became vacant for a moment, but then said sure, like it was no problem.

She readied herself at the keys, taking in a slight breath.

Her arms became loose then, owned by something else, and she started coaxing an impossibly effortless melody, her fingertips, chipped with polish, twinkling along the whites and blacks.

I watched Zoe rise and fall with the music, hypnotized by the bones writhing in her back, by the way her eyes scrunched together as though the sheet music was imprinted on her lids.

When she reached the chorus, she looked up to me, the music suspended between us, and I knew she was inviting me to sing. And for her, I did, my voice finding me easier than it had at the bar.

On the piano, *Time After Time* never sounded so sombre, and when it was all over and I was trying not to cry, Zoe turned to me and said, "This is my favourite place to be, Clare. The only place I can disappear and be fully seen at the same time."

And how fortunate I felt that she let me visit her there.

"Do you have a place like that?"

nine

So here is how my night with Zoe would come to an end, passing a cheap bottle of merlot between us on top of Montpelier Hill, the capital a vast and glittering circuit board of reds and oranges in the distance.

"You know," Zoe said there on the grass, leaning back on her elbows as though she was on a sunbed in Spain. "When I asked you to take me to your favourite place, Clare, I had something a little more local in mind."

It had been a thirty-minute taxi ride to the bottom of the viewpoint, and I was just the right amount of glazed to ignore the soaring fare calculator. Zoe, on the other hand, seemed to grow more and more concerned when the urban landscape receded around her. Out here, the roads were narrower, the signs of life few and far between.

"What, did you think I was going to take you to Temple Bar, Zoe?"

She laughed, made a face like: fair, fair.

Though we were both freezing up there, it was something we pretended not to notice in one another, gravely aware that acknowledging our trembling or the yawns that we passed back and forth might spell the end of our one night engagement. And I don't think either of us were ready for that, least of all me.

Rubbing hard on my bare legs, as if to rid them of the goose bumps, I made the mistake of debriefing Zoe on the hilltops dark past.

Montpelier Hill was a place where history seemed to blur with chilling legends, the summit crowned with the ancient stone ruins of a hunting lodge, more commonly known to Dubliners as the Hell Fire Club.

When I finished telling her about how the burnt-out relic was believed to be crawling with vengeful spirits, visited by the devil himself, and was, allegedly, the site of countless sacrifices, Zoe looked at me as though I'd unwittingly dragged her into a horror movie and said:

"Is that what you've got planned for me then? A sacrifice?"

For a moment I glared at her and, with the torch from my phone shining between us, I must have looked horrifying because she glanced over both her shoulders and then whacked my arm when I broke into laughter, telling me to *eff off!*

"Relax, Zoe" I said, downing some wine. "They're very strict on their 'Virgins Only' rule, anyway." I lowered my face when I said *virgins only* and, though it was the kind of remark that implied the existence of a more versed friendship, one I definitely told with a sliver of uncertainty, she shrieked nevertheless, holding her smile behind her hand.

That was something I caught her doing a lot, and I wondered if she was insecure about her mouth. The idea that Zoe would be insecure about any part of her body was as unbelievable as it was offensive. I bet whenever she complained about her appearance to her friends, they rolled their eyes and told her she was crazy, because that's what I'd do.

It might be nice to have a particular anxiety in common with her, I thought, but that could also be a treacherous alliance. When we were teenagers, Roisin and I had bonded over our mutual disdain for our bodies, regularly sending each other *Thinspo* posts on Tumblr and swapping our daily calorie figures each night like a grotesque game of Top Trumps.

In hindsight, our twisted support for each other during that time was actually detrimental to our health. Even more damaging was when Roisin decided to "grow out of it" and began to embrace her body, leaving me behind to shrivel on my own.

I once spent six weeks in hospital, and when Roisin visited me on a Wednesday afternoon, she said, "Dude, I thought we stopped doing all that?"

Zoe waved her hand for the bottle of wine and then asked why I enjoyed coming here so much. I didn't know how to answer that right away because I wasn't sure Montpelier Hill was even my favourite place to go, or if such a place even existed for me anymore.

If I was being honest with her back in Connolly, when she'd asked me to take her to my favourite place, we probably would've ended up in my bed at home, the covers pulled over our head, but that might've been a little depressing.

There definitely *was* a time when this land was sacred to me, the kind of place that brought me the same comfort that sitting at a piano brought Zoe. Whether it was with Jack or Roisin here, I always loved it and how it reminded me of being back home in Kerry – without the actual hassle of having to go there and visit my fractured parents.

However, the last time I'd trekked up that hill, cutting through the shortcut in the trail that Jack had shown me, the same off-the-map track he'd called me his girlfriend on for the first time, I found that Montpellier Hill had been completely deconsecrated to me.

If I wasn't such a wimp that night, I could've followed my grief all the way down.

"Isn't it obvious?" I replied, looking back out over the bay.

Regardless of how I felt about it now, the views were unmatched, particularly at night when the sky was that clear, peppered with so many stars it was as if a bag of sugar had been spilled over it. I made a point of watching Zoe's reaction when we finally reached the top that night, witnessed the worry on her face melt away when she saw all the lights.

I was so jealous that she was seeing it all for the first time, but also completely grateful that I got to be the one to show her.

"Did she like it here too?" Zoe asked, and I didn't have to question who she was referring to. Roisin was the only actual ghost on that hill.

"No," I said, as though there was a funny memory behind it. And there were, but too many of them to pinpoint and share. "She must've come here a hundred times with me, though. I think she considered it penance for all the art galleries she made me go to."

Zoe smiled. "You sound like you were a right pair, you two."

Hearing that stung, the hefty *were* sinking the statement, but I didn't hold it against her. I just took another long gulp from the wine that was nearly gone and said, "You remind me of her in some way."

Zoe sat up then so that she was mirroring me and waited for me to continue.

"I don't know," I said, even though I really did know. It was all I really knew. "It's something about the way you carry yourself about the world, like you know exactly who you are. It's quite remarkable. And a little annoying, actually."

She stayed quiet for a moment, as though translating my words into a language she could understand, like: hold on, I don't speak sorrow. I archived the expression on her face. It was one that made me think she'd never thought of herself in that way before and kind of liked the idea of it, of being remarkable to someone.

Deep down, we all love being noticed, I think.

"What was she like?" Zoe asked quietly. "If you don't mind me asking."

Summing up Roisin would be like trying to give context to a person watching EastEnders for the very first time; I didn't know where to begin.

If I wanted to tell her the truth, I'd tell Zoe that working Roisin out was sometimes like trying to solve a jigsaw with no box to guide you, that she was flawed in only the ways her best friend could notice. I'd tell her that she often gave people a reason to dislike her in case they found one on their own, that she was so afraid of being left behind she decided to beat everyone to the punch instead.

Later, long after Zoe was gone, I'd compile a list of all the things I could've told her about Roisin if I'd had the time, if I was faster at marrying my words and emotions and wasn't so terrified of their bastard, but there, I just said, "She was a blessing. In every way a person can be without being a fantasy."

I'd said this mostly because Roisin herself once told me, after Jack and I broke up the first time over something I can't even recall now, that people come into your life for one of two distinct reasons. Either they're a blessing, she said, or a lesson. And I was sure, right down to my marrow, that she was the former, despite how she'd left.

"You must miss her," Zoe replied.

"Always," I admitted at once, my hand on my face, then running through my hair. There was one more sip of wine before I could go on. "It's weird because sometimes I'll expect her to just walk in like this has all been some kind of nightmare. Or I'll hear a noise in the other room and for a brief moment I'll think to myself, oh it's just Roisin. But then it hits me all over again. And then I don't know what to do with all that..." I paused to find the right word. "... with all that space."

Zoe nudged me a little then, as though to remind me of her presence. “Well, that’s the thing about space, Clare,” she said. “There’s so many ways to fill it.”

I remember immediately thinking that, in theory, this was profound and so true, but putting it in to practice was a whole other daunting idea.

Yes, I could wake up tomorrow and start gathering the things I’d abandoned this year, the book that might be the best work I’ve ever done, the friendships I still wanted but had neglected to the point of decay, the trip to New York I’d been planning since last summer but had to set aside when my supposed travel buddy took a more permanent vacation, etcetera, etcetera.

And I knew that all of these things would still be there, waiting to be exhumed, and that they’d undoubtedly fill the space. But at what cost? The more distractions I used to plug this hole, the further the water would rise, and then I’d be even more removed from Roisin.

It’s us and all the space in-between, she’d told me. But I didn’t want any space in between us. I wanted her here, always and forever. Faulty parts and all. And I'm sure that, if she were to come back, if I could just see her once more, I'd forgive her of everything.

"What if I can't do it, Zoe?" I said. "What if I can't fill that space?"

Zoe took my hand in hers then, and I felt something kindle there, as if we were nurturing a tiny flame between our palms. For a moment she was very still, the trees below us the sound of undulating waves, which allowed me to fully prepare for what she said next.

"I think you've already started, Clare."

When I look back on that night, next to Zoe on Montpelier Hill, I'm not sure I can determine the exact moment I kissed her, but I think it was somewhere around there, the thought coming to me fully formed.

The world turned its back on us for five enchanted seconds, the most colourful moment in a year of blacks and greys. With no remarkable demand, my hand found her face and held her in it, as if to physically hold on to the moment and keep it from slipping away before I could imprint it in my brain.

Though there was no Hollywood fireworks or tingles in my most delicate parts, it obliterated every whirling thought I'd had, our breathing becoming one, in and out as gentle as sleep, as if some people were specifically made to be a living organism with another.

When the kiss ended, Zoe whispered against my mouth, "Is that something you used to do with Roisin?" And I tried to muster something in reply, but it was too hard. So I nodded a *yes* instead, felt her forehead brush against my own.

My biggest worry was that she was going to walk away after I kissed her, but she didn't. She just returned to leaning on her elbows and took in the view. When Roisin had kissed me first, we were sixteen years old and I couldn't face her for a week, which proved difficult because we carpooled to school every day with my mother.

Though I was certain she didn't possess the same complex feelings I did, feelings I wasn't ashamed of but hadn't probed too much in my life, Zoe seemed very content lying there, watching as the dark sky began to dissolve, Dublin Bay coming out of the shadows.

The birds soon started their morning song, the assaulting breeze winding down, and it was then that Zoe coolly determined, "You're not as hopeless as you think you are, Clare."

I'd laughed at that, a bit self-deprecatingly, and began picking at the slick grass for something to do with my hands. "Do you not think, no?"

"No, I reckon you're going to be okay." Her conviction was so smooth, I even started to humour it. "Actually, I think you might *want* to be okay. But you're just afraid of it, like the very idea of being happy again terrifies you."

It would take me weeks to realize what Zoe said that morning was mostly true. Being happy in a world without Roisin meant accepting that she was gone, and that I had been blind to her pain. How on earth was I to approach that with no fear?

"I just don't think I know who I am anymore, Zoe," I confessed, letting the loose pieces of grass roll off my palm. "Like, when you lose a parent you're an orphan, or when your spouse dies, you're a widow. But what do you call it when your best friend kills themselves? They don't even have a name for that."

Zoe bent her knees and pushed herself up then, did a big stretch after being on the hard ground for so long. The backside of her dungarees were wet, stamped with a thousand gashes from the grass, and she had two dark patches that were glued to her buttocks.

"Well, you're the writer here," she said, shoulders slumping. "Why don't you come up with one?"

Sometime after that, she left, and if I had known it was going to be the last time I'd ever see her, I might've watched her go, memorizing every edge of her body. But I didn't. I let her walk away as if tomorrow was guaranteed, as if there'd be thousand more nights and ample time to study her.

Maybe I'd never learn.

She'd asked me to come with her, but I told her I wanted to stick around to watch the sunrise, if that was okay with her. It had been a while since I'd done that and, for some reason I couldn't make sense of, I felt that it was of the utmost importance that I did.

"Will you be all right by yourself?" Zoe said before leaving.

"I think so."

And that was that.

When she was gone, I brought my knees to my chest and wrapped my arms around them, holding myself as though I might fall apart.

The sun didn't rear its head until after four in the morning, but it was worth the wait in the end, it's ascent into the sky slow and magnificent, transforming the powdered world, the grass and still trees, the stone lodge, the hills and the valley, into a golden oasis, the city blurring below me in a silvery haze.

It's invigorating rays beamed across the land; I could almost hear them hum. When it got too bright to look at anymore, I closed my eyes and knew she would be there. The beacon. The supernova. But at least I could still see her, I thought.

ten

When I got back home later that morning, Zoe was already gone.

I stalled in the doorway, like I'd inadvertently walked into the wrong apartment, and called out her name. The silence seemed to press back against me there, an invisible entity in my hallway that, for the first time in a while, I greeted with disdain.

"Zoe?" I said again. "Are you here?"

In the spare room, I found that everything inside was exactly the way I'd left it the morning before, the bedsheets unsullied and creaseless, like how they might be in an Ikea or my mother's house, the air still blithe with that cheap, lavender freshener.

I once felt like the only way to know my guests was through the mess they left behind, but what was I to take away from Zoe when it was as if she'd never even been here?

In my bedroom then, I put my phone on charge and watched it with an intense anticipation, but no check-out notification or review ever came through on Bunker. And, without Zoe's number, or even a surname to search on Facebook, I had no way of getting in touch with her myself.

She was gone, as quickly and peculiarly as she'd appeared, leaving her mark not with forgotten socks under the bed or a bottle of wine on the counter, but in other, more ambiguous ways, the kind of residue that would take weeks to discover.

For the rest of the morning, I didn't quite know what to do with myself. I was unusually agitated; too tired to sleep, too hungry to eat. I kept wandering in and out of rooms with no apparent motive, only to come back into them minutes later, just as aimless and even more frustrated.

Had she really left without saying goodbye?

Around noon, I realized I was still in the clothes I'd thrown up in and felt rotten, so I decided to take a hot shower and wash away the grime that can only be earned from a memorable night in the city.

It was in the shower that I realized Roisin had been wrong about something. People aren't exclusively one thing, either lessons or blessings. Sometimes they are both.

Returning to my room, feeling somewhat lighter than I had before, I dried off and slipped into a pair of comfortable shorts, the kind that made me think I'd subconsciously resorted to a day of idleness.

I had nothing to put on top of me, though. All of my t-shirts and sweaters were dirty, hiding like rodents in the corner of my room. I'd have to tackle the laundry tomorrow, I told myself, but for now I'd make use of whatever was in my bottom drawer.

Roisin's shirt was there, a green flannel she'd salvaged from a St Vincent De Paul's. It was two sizes too big for anyone and was missing a bunch of buttons, but she'd loved the thing, wore it for one week straight during her sustainability phase.

When her parents came to clear out her room, silently packing all of her belongings into unmarked boxes, it was the only item I actually asked to keep, even though I felt bad doing so, like I was stealing one of the very few pieces that remained of their daughter.

They were happy to let me have it, however, and left the painting behind as well.

I never dreamed of putting it on, instead figured it might be better to preserve it in some way, saving it for when it got especially difficult and I needed to be reminded of what she used to smell like. But it felt safe to wear it then, and so I pulled it out of its tomb and threw it around me, bringing the sleeves to my face for one last reminder.

Later that night, I'd surrendered to my bed with bleary eyes, but my mind wouldn't let me rest. Thoughts and musings and emotions were fighting for attention, for release, and it took me a while to recognise that alluring sensation.

Once it became clear to me, I shot out of bed again and went to my desk with the exhilaration of a jackpot winner.

Maybe there were many ways to fill the space, like Zoe said. And maybe one day I'd learn them all. But only one of them was speaking to me now, the curtain to that other realm flapping open, inviting me to slip inside. No brick wall this time.

I opened my MacBook, brought up my manuscript.

Go.

the story continues…

FALLING INTO PLACE

coming soon

stay up to date with news and updates from the author on instagram @shaun__powell

shaun powell

the thing about space

acknowledgements

With so many people contributing to this story in one form or another, I'd just like to give a blanket thank you to all of my friends and family who have been so patient and encouraging during its creation.

Work on *The Thing About Space* originally began in 2016, a short story about a break-up that I never intended to share with anyone. That story became the unintentional basis for Clare and Zoe's adventure around Dublin and, though it approaches it in a different way, still covers the themes from the original.

This novella is incredibly precious to me and has been a welcome distraction during these uncertain times. I really hope you've enjoyed reading it.

Shaun

the thing about space

Printed in Great Britain
by Amazon